Just a Coincidence?

Elizabeth wrote down the first number that popped into her head. "OK," she said, turning to Jessica.

Jessica frowned for a moment and chewed her lip. Finally she blew out her breath. "Three hundred and twenty-eight," she said with conviction.

Elizabeth felt her heart jump. Wordlessly she held up the napkin.

"Three hundred and twenty-eight!" Mandy Miller squealed.

Randy blinked in surprise. "Wow!"

Janet Howell looked taken aback.

Elizabeth swallowed nervously. It was a coincidence. Just another coincidence. Wasn't it?

SWEET VALLEY TWINS titles, published by Bantam Books.
Ask your bookseller for titles you have missed:

SWEET VALLEY TWINS

Psychic Sisters

Written by
Jamie Suzanne

Created by
FRANCINE PASCAL

BANTAM BOOKS

TORONTO • NEW YORK • LONDON • SYDNEY • AUCKLAND

PSYCHIC SISTERS
A BANTAM BOOK 0 553 40686 8

Originally published in U.S.A. by Bantam Skylark Books

First publication in Great Britain

PRINTING HISTORY
Bantam edition published 1993

Sweet Valley High and Sweet Valley Twins are registered
trademarks of Francine Pascal.

Conceived by Francine Pascal.

Produced by Daniel Weiss Associates, Inc., 33 West 17th Street,
New York, NY 10011

All rights reserved.

Bantam Books are published by Transworld Publishers Ltd.,
61–63 Uxbridge Road, Ealing, London W5 5SA,
in Australia by Transworld Publishers (Australia) Pty. Ltd.,
15–25 Helles Avenue, Moorebank, NSW 2170,
and in New Zealand by Transworld Publishers (N.Z.) Ltd.,
3 William Pickering Drive, Albany, Auckland.

Printed and bound in Great Britain by
Cox & Wyman Ltd., Reading, Berks.

One

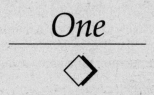

"Jessica," Mr. Wakefield whispered. "Are you awake?"

With superhuman effort, Jessica Wakefield managed to lift the lid of one eye, and saw her father peering down at her. She tried to speak, but she was too sleepy. Jessica let the heavy lid fall shut.

Dimly, she heard another voice in the background. "Thanks for tuning in tonight. We'll return to our special surprise feature after a word from our sponsor, Corny—"

Click.

The room was suddenly silent. When Jessica opened her eye again, she saw her father tiptoeing away from the television.

He turned and cast a last look at Jessica and her twin sister, Elizabeth, who were asleep on the living-room floor in their sleeping bags. Then he tiptoed toward the stairs.

Jessica tried to say good night, but she was already slipping back into her dream . . . zzzzz.

Steven Wakefield rushed into the living room and then skidded to a stop. Amazing. Elizabeth and Jessica were still asleep. That was pretty normal for Jessica, but Elizabeth asleep at eleven o'clock?

"Yes. That's right. Three hundred and twenty-eight people. A very large group . . ." he heard his mother's voice from the kitchen. "I'd like to get the details set now, because I'll be out of town at a convention next week . . . Yes. I think the Washington Room would be perfect." What an incredibly boring morning. His sisters were sound asleep and his mother had been on the phone for almost an hour. He couldn't watch the basketball game on TV and he couldn't call his best friend, Joe Howell.

Steven stepped over Jessica's sleeping bag and reached for the TV section of the newspaper, which was on the floor next to her.

". . . It's a black-tie dinner," he heard his mother saying. "The California Interior Designers' Association holds it annually, and I'm serving as the chairwoman this year. That's right. On the fifteenth. That's right. No, that room is too small; we need to hold the dinner in the Washington Room this year."

Steven flipped through the TV section and

sighed. This was his fourth trip into the living room to see if his mother was off the phone. She had been talking to the same guy for almost an hour, going over and over the information for some banquet she was organizing.

Steven sighed grumpily. Why was it taking the guy so long to get all the information straight? After listening to his mother's end of the conversation, even Steven knew the details of the dumb party by heart—a black-tie dinner for 328 people in the George Washington Room.

He looked down at his sisters. Jessica cracked an eye open, then buried her head under her pillow. He was really tempted to turn on the TV. But his mother had told him he had to wait until the twins woke up. She wanted them to sleep as late as they could, since they'd been up late watching the Teen Movie Marathon.

Steven hadn't wanted to watch it. It was fine for his sisters. They were in sixth grade. But he was a freshman at Sweet Valley High, and the Teen Movie Marathon was way too immature for somebody in high school. And he couldn't stand listening to his sisters squeal over Johnny Buck.

Johnny Buck was a rock musician and movie star, and the twins were both big fans.

A few feet away from Jessica, Elizabeth stirred slightly.

Good. Maybe they'd wake up soon and he could watch TV.

Mrs. Wakefield's voice continued to float into the living room. "No. I don't think they can comfortably accommodate a group that size, which is why I think the Washington Room is preferable." Was this guy some kind of idiot? Steven wondered.

"Uh huh. OK. But will it be ready by then? Yes. I'll hold," Mrs. Wakefield continued patiently. "Excuse me? The twenty-eighth? The fifteenth would really be better, but let me get back to you tomorrow, when I've consulted the other members of the committee."

Steven looked down at Elizabeth again. She had sunk back into a deep sleep. He looked hopefully over at Jessica and pulled the pillow off of her head.

"Go away, Steven," she muttered without opening her eyes.

Steven looked at them and began to laugh. His sisters looked even more identical in their sleep than they did when they were awake. They both had light-blue nightgowns, messy blond hair, and were sleeping with their mouths open.

But they were easy to tell apart when they were awake. They had completely different personalities and interests. Jessica was part of a club of gossipy girls called the Unicorns. Elizabeth and Steven both thought they were pretty silly. Elizabeth spent most of her time working on the sixth-grade newspaper, which Steven and Jessica both thought was kind of boring.

Steven darted a look toward the kitchen and saw that his mother had her back to the open door. Very carefully, he reached out and nudged Elizabeth with his foot.

Elizabeth stirred.

Steven nudged a little harder, then quickly pulled his foot away. Elizabeth opened her eyes and groaned. She looked around in confusion. "Why am I in the living room?" she asked sleepily.

Steven smiled. "Because you guys were going to stay up all night watching the Teen Movie Marathon. Did you make it through all five movies?"

Elizabeth blinked and rubbed her eyes. "I didn't."

Jessica's lids fluttered and then opened. "Arrgg," she said sleepily.

Elizabeth reached over and shook her shoulder. "Jessica. Wake up."

Jessica sat up and rubbed her eyes. "What time is it?"

"Almost eleven," Steven answered. "You guys have been dead all morning." He looked at Jessica and laughed. "Serious bed-head, Jess."

"Did you make it through all five movies?" Elizabeth asked Jessica.

Jessica rubbed her head sleepily and yawned. "Uh-uh. I don't know when I fell asleep, but I never saw the Surprise Teen Feature."

"Darn," Elizabeth said. "Did you even stay awake long enough to find out what it was?"

Jessica shook her head.

Steven grinned. "I guess that means you didn't catch the Teen Movie Trivia Quiz."

"No," Jessica said in a disappointed voice. "And I'll bet I knew all the answers, too."

"Oh yeah?" Steven said. "Why's that?"

Jessica shrugged and pointed to her temple. "I don't know. 'Cause I'm psychic."

"Thank you, Mr. Peters. Thank you so much. I'll get a confirmation letter and a check for the deposit to you," Mrs. Wakefield was saying into the phone when the girls walked into the kitchen a few minutes later. "Yes . . . Thank you very much. Goodbye." Mrs. Wakefield hung up the phone and smiled at the girls. "Good morning!"

"Good morning," Elizabeth answered.

"Mmmmmmm," Jessica mumbled sleepily, slumping into a chair at the kitchen table.

"You girls must be hungry. It's past eleven o'clock."

Elizabeth went over to the pantry and stared wearily at the row of cereal boxes that lined the shelf. Finally she selected one and took it to the table.

She poured out two bowls of cereal and shoved one toward Jessica. "Wake up and eat," she said.

Jessica looked down curiously into the bowl. "That's really weird," she commented. "I woke up thinking about Corny-O's this morning."

Elizabeth shrugged. "Really? Maybe *I'm* psychic.

For some reason I woke up thinking about them too. And I haven't had Corny-O's in ages."

"Who's psychic?" Mr. Wakefield asked, coming into the kitchen just in time to hear the end of their conversation.

"Both of us," Elizabeth said with a laugh.

Jessica shook her head. "I still can't believe I missed my big chance to be on television and be famous just because I fell asleep before the Teen Movie Trivia Quiz."

"You'll get another chance someday," Elizabeth assured her. "Something tells me your big chance to be famous is just around the corner."

"Oh yeah? What makes you think so?"

"I'm psychic!" Elizabeth grinned. "Remember?"

I wish the people in this family would find someplace to sleep besides the living room, Steven thought irritably as he walked into the house late that afternoon. His father was sound asleep on the sofa.

Steven began to tiptoe to the kitchen, trying hard not to make any noise. He successfully navigated his way around the overstuffed wing chair, but when he passed the coffee table, he caught his leg on the edge of a pile of books and magazines.

CRASH!

The books and magazines fell to the floor and Mr. Wakefield sat straight up with a startled *"Hey!"*

"Sorry, Dad."

Mr. Wakefield blinked in confusion at Steven for a moment. Then he grinned. "Guess I was asleep."

"You sure were," Steven said. "Are you sick or something? You never sleep in the afternoon."

Mr. Wakefield laughed and smoothed his hair down. "No, I feel fine. I guess I just stayed up too late watching the Teen Movie Marathon."

"You're kidding!" Steven laughed. "I didn't know you were a teen-movie fan."

Mr. Wakefield began to straighten up the newspapers that were strewn around the sofa. "When I came downstairs last night to check on Elizabeth and Jessica, there was a movie on and I sort of got hooked watching it. It was the surprise feature and it had Johnny Buck in it. I saw the trivia quiz, too. I tried to wake the girls, but they were too far gone." He laughed. "Don't tell them or I'll never hear the end of it."

"*You* watched the surprise teen feature?" Steven exclaimed. He laughed even harder. "Wasn't it kind of dumb?"

"Actually, it was sort of interesting. Johnny Buck played a young French aristocrat who tries to save the girl he loves from the guillotine."

"How did it end?"

Mr. Wakefield yawned. "I don't know. I finally had to give up because I got tired of watching so many commercials. They must have had twelve commercials every ten minutes. How often can you listen to that Corny-O's jingle before you lose your mind?"

Two

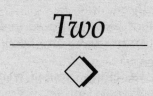

"I keep telling her not to feel bad," Elizabeth said. "From what I hear, *nobody* made it all the way through the Teen Movie Marathon."

"I'll bet nobody else knew all the answers to the trivia quiz, either," Jessica said glumly.

It was Monday morning, and the twins were walking out of their first-period class with Amy Sutton, Elizabeth's best friend.

"I fell asleep in the middle of the first movie," Amy Sutton admitted sheepishly. "And Elizabeth's right. Nobody I've talked to saw the surprise feature or heard the quiz. Nobody managed to stay up that late."

Jessica yawned and Elizabeth smiled. "I'll bet nobody else tried as hard as Jessica. Too bad they don't give prizes for trying."

"Speaking of prizes," Amy said. "Did you know that the first prize in the school talent show is a pair of season tickets to the L.A. Lions' soccer games? Are you two going to enter it?"

"Yeah," Jessica said excitedly. "I'm definitely going to enter the show."

Elizabeth shot her a surprised look. "I thought you said you didn't have any talent that people would pay to see."

"That was yesterday," Jessica responded. "I'm feeling more self-confident today. I'm just going to have to figure out what my talent is. I've still got a few days before the deadline to sign up." Suddenly her eyebrows shot up. "Hey! Maybe we can do our pea-pong routine."

Elizabeth laughed.

A few months before, Elizabeth and Jessica had been picked to appear on the *Staying Up With Bob* TV show, which featured a segment called "Stupid Stunts." Jessica and Elizabeth had played a silly game of Ping-Pong. But instead of using a Ping-Pong ball, they had used green peas. The stunt had been a big success and the girls had gotten lots of laughs. For weeks, the kids at school had treated them like celebrities.

"I don't think we should do our pea-pong routine," Elizabeth said. "This talent show isn't a stupid-stunt type of thing. It's a real talent show. They're selling tickets to it to raise money for the Sweet Valley Children's Hospital. The kids who are going to be in the show should have real talent. They'll play the violin and stuff like that."

"Amy's going to be in it," Jessica countered.

"*I* have a real talent," Amy said hotly. "I'm going to do a tumbling routine to music. I've been practicing it for three weeks."

Jessica pursed her lips. "I guess. But if Ellen Riteman can actually get herself billed as the main attraction, it can't be that hard to get in."

"Ellen Riteman is going to be the main attraction?" Elizabeth exclaimed. "What's her talent?"

"She doesn't have any," Jessica said sourly. "She just thinks she does. She's going to sing, but she's a terrible singer."

"Then how did she get in the show?" Amy asked. "And how did she get top billing?"

Jessica twirled a strand of hair thoughtfully. "Well, her mom *is* head of the parent group that's organizing the show." Jessica shrugged. "That might have something to do with it."

Elizabeth laughed. "There's one mystery solved."

"Hey, maybe you two can work up some kind of sister act," Amy suggested as they stopped at Jessica's locker. "You know, take advantage of the twin thing."

"We'd love to work up a sister act," Elizabeth said. "But we just haven't been able to come up with any talent that really seems worth showing."

"*Yet!*" Jessica said with conviction.

Amy laughed and bent over to tie her shoe. As she did, a book fell out of her bag.

Elizabeth leaned over to pick up the book. "*Mayflower Diary*," she read. "That sounds pretty interesting."

"*Interesting?*" Jessica repeated incredulously.

"It's for social studies," Amy explained, taking the book from Elizabeth. "For the research paper we were assigned last week. I thought I'd do mine on the early-American settlers. What are you guys going to write about?"

"The French Revolution," Jessica and Elizabeth answered at exactly the same time.

They turned to stare at each other in surprise.

"That's strange. What made you pick the French Revolution?" Elizabeth asked.

Jessica shrugged. "I have no idea. I never thought about it before in my life. But I woke up this morning with the idea."

"That's kind of spooky," Elizabeth said. "I woke up thinking about it too."

Jessica felt a little shiver of goose bumps along her spine. "This is really weird," she said softly. Her eyes widened. "It's just like the Corny-O's."

Amy laughed. "Did I miss something? What do Corny-O's have to do with the French Revolution?"

Elizabeth giggled and then quickly told Amy about how she had poured them both a bowl of Corny-O's cereal yesterday, and it turned out that both had awakened with Corny-O's on their minds.

"We're psychic!" Jessica said, feeling a little flicker of excitement in her stomach. "We're definitely psychic."

"It's going to be sooooo embarrassing," Mandy Miller groaned that afternoon at lunch.

Jessica sat with her friends from the Unicorn Club at their regular table, which they called the Unicorner.

Tamara Chase scanned the front of the cafeteria to make sure Ellen Riteman was still waiting in the lunch line. "Ellen's going to make us look bad in front of the entire school."

"Janet, isn't there anything you can do about it?" Mandy Miller asked. "Ellen sounds like a sick cow when she sings. It's going to make the whole club look really stupid."

Janet Howell held up her hands for silence. Janet was an eighth-grader and president of the Unicorn Club, and as far as Jessica was concerned, she took her presidential duties a little too seriously sometimes. "I've tried to drop one or two *subtle* hints, but she just refuses to pick up on them. Ellen is determined to sing at the talent show." She gazed seriously at Mandy and Tamara. "It's up to you two to salvage the honor of the club with your act."

"But we're just lip-synchers," Tamara argued. "And Mandy and I are alternates. We don't even get to go on unless somebody drops out of the show and they need an extra act to fill in."

Janet sighed. "Everybody wish for a miracle, then. Maybe something will happen to keep Ellen from going on." She looked around the table. "I think we need to call a Unicorn meeting for this afternoon," she said. "It might not be a bad idea for us all to discuss what we're going to wear on the night of the talent show. There will be tons of people there, and since Ellen is going to be such a big embarrassment, we can at least look good."

"Tamara and I can't make it this afternoon," Mandy said. "We've got to practice our lip-synching act."

"Fine. Practice all you can," Janet said. "We'll talk about wardrobe tomorrow at lunch."

Jessica wished for the twentieth time that she had some kind of extra-special talent that would get her into the talent show. Then *she* could salvage the honor of the Unicorns.

And she'd also have something more exciting to do this afternoon than researching her social-studies paper in the library.

The French Revolution was pretty gruesome when you got right down to it, Jessica decided that afternoon as she sat in the library researching her paper—all those French aristocrats getting their heads chopped off and everything.

She gazed down at the illustration in the book she was reading. It was a reproduction of an engraving from the period, showing a young man with a ponytail being taken to the guillotine in the back of a rickety cart. "Remember Me Well" was the title of the engraving. He looked sort of like Johnny Buck, Jessica decided.

Jessica fidgeted in her seat. Reading about the French Revolution was depressing. And it made her sad to think that somebody who looked like Johnny Buck had gotten his head cut off all those years ago. What had made her think she wanted to do her paper on the French Revolution? And what had given Elizabeth the same idea? It sure was weird. This wasn't the kind of subject that she'd usually choose. "Makeup Through the Ages" was more her speed.

Jessica looked up and saw Randy Mason sitting on the other side of the table.

He must have felt Jessica's eyes on him, because he glanced up from his magazine briefly. "Hi, Jessica," he said. Then he quickly turned his attention back to his magazine.

"Hi," Jessica responded.

Randy Mason was Sweet Valley Middle School's resident science nerd. The Unicorns thought he was a total geek. But he and Jessica had been in a special science class together called SOAR!—for Science Offers Awesome Rewards—and they had sort of become friends. He was actually pretty funny if you were into jokes about electrons and quarks and stuff.

Jessica darted a look at him. She was so sick of

studying, she was dying for a distraction. But Randy's nose was buried in his magazine. She took a quick look at the cover and gasped. "Psychic Phenomena: Fact or Fiction?" a big headline read.

Jessica bit her lip. Another coincidence.

"Ahem! Ahem!" Jessica cleared her throat as loudly as possible, hoping to get Randy's attention. But Randy appeared to be totally absorbed in his magazine.

"AHEM! AHEM!" Jessica tried again even more loudly.

Randy didn't look up.

Jessica reached over and tapped his arm.

Randy jumped in his seat and dropped his magazine. "Geez, you scared me," he said. He retrieved his magazine and pushed his glasses back up on his nose.

"Sorry," Jessica said. "Why are you so jumpy?"

Randy tapped his magazine. "Some of this stuff is really spooky," he said. "I'm reading about a guy with ESP. He knew that a murder was about to take place. He kept trying to tell the police, but of course, they wouldn't believe him. So he had to try to stop the murderer himself."

"How come the police didn't believe him?" Jessica asked.

"Because most people don't believe in stuff like that," Randy said. "Psychic phenomena is a pretty new field of study. Some people think it's for real, but some people think it's baloney."

"Do you think it's real?" Jessica asked, her heart beating faster.

"I do," Randy said.

"How would you know if you were . . . well . . . you know, *psychic?*"

Randy scratched his head thoughtfully. "I guess you'd have premonitions. Or you'd know things that you couldn't know unless you were receiving psychic messages."

"You mean you could read people's minds?"

Randy frowned. "I don't know about that. But you'd probably be able to get *some* insight into other people's thoughts and feelings."

"Are you interested in psychic stuff?" Jessica asked.

"Yeah. My uncle got me interested. He's totally into it. He's a documentary filmmaker in Los Angeles, and, as a matter of fact, he's working on a major film about psychic phenomena right now."

Jessica's heart began to thud. Just yesterday Elizabeth had said that Jessica's big chance to be famous was right around the corner. And now, here was Randy telling her that his uncle was working on a film about psychic phenomena. Put that together with the Corny-O's and the French Revolution and it all added up to one thing: *Jessica and Elizabeth were psychic. And they were about to be famous!*

"Randy," Jessica said eagerly. "You should tell your uncle about me and Elizabeth."

"What about you and Elizabeth?"

Jessica looked around to be sure they weren't being overheard. "We're psychic," she whispered.

Randy began to laugh.

"It's true," Jessica insisted.

"Yeah. I bet."

Jessica quickly told him about the Corny-O's and the French Revolution. She didn't mention what Elizabeth had said about Jessica's becoming famous, because she didn't want Randy to think she was making it up so she could get into his uncle's film.

Randy gave Jessica a skeptical look. "Listen, Jessica. Those are just a couple of coincidences. Stuff like that happens to people all the time. It doesn't mean you're psychic."

Randy began to stuff his magazine into his book bag. He looked so unimpressed and superior, it made Jessica furious. Randy Mason was a nerd. *She* was a Unicorn. How dare he tell her that her psychic experiences were just coincidences!

"Well," she said. "There is that time I saved Elizabeth's life."

Randy's eyes widened. "Huh?"

That was better. Randy had begun to look interested.

"It happened when we were really little," she said breathlessly. "I suddenly had an overwhelming sense that Elizabeth was in trouble. Terrible, terrible trouble. I sensed that she was locked in the basement. Sure enough, when my parents went down there to look, they found her."

"And . . . ?"

"And what?"

"That's it? That's the whole story?"

"Isn't that enough?"

Randy rolled his eyes. "That's not much of a story. I mean, anybody with common sense might have decided to look in the basement for a missing kid."

Jessica frowned. Maybe he was right. It sure wasn't as dramatic as getting a premonition about a murder. Maybe she should exaggerate a little.

"Well, the basement was flooded with water," Jessica added tentatively.

"You mean a couple of inches?"

"No! I mean a real flood. The whole time I was getting those feelings that she was in trouble, I had a suffocating feeling—like I couldn't breathe. When my parents finally went down into the basement, the water was up to Elizabeth's chin and she was standing on her tiptoes to keep from drowning."

"You really did save her life, then?" Randy asked eagerly.

Jessica nodded solemnly.

Randy shook his head in amazement. "So the whole time Elizabeth was afraid she was going to drown, you were having a suffocating feeling. Wow! I've heard that twins are sometimes psychic like that. You know, one twin in Colorado breaks a leg and the other twin in Maine feels a pain in the exact same spot."

"That's the kind of thing that happens to me and Elizabeth all the time," Jessica lied.

Randy scratched his head. "I *will* tell my uncle about you guys."

It was all Jessica could do not to scream. Wait till Elizabeth heard about this!

But then she remembered that most of her story had been a big lie. Hmmm. On second thought, maybe she wouldn't tell Elizabeth anything about it just yet.

Elizabeth was sitting on her bed that evening checking over her math homework, when suddenly the door burst open and Jessica came flying in.

"Don't tell me," Jessica said, pressing her fingertips to her temples. "You're thinking about fried chicken, aren't you?"

"Yes," Elizabeth answered with a laugh. "But that's because Mom's making it downstairs. Is dinner ready?"

Jessica sat down on the bed. "I don't know. Let's see if we can read Mom's mind from here. Concentrate."

"Jessica! Elizabeth!" they heard Mrs. Wakefield call from downstairs. "Dinner!"

"Darn!" Jessica said. "How are we ever going to develop our psychic powers if people just come right out and tell us what's on their mind?"

Elizabeth laughed. "Unfortunately, I haven't

gotten any psychic readings all day. I think we may have to face the fact that we aren't psychic after all."

"Come on, Lizzie. Don't give up so easily," Jessica argued. "Just think how useful it would be." She grinned. "Useful for me, anyway. I'd never have to study again. I could just read the answers from your mind."

Three

"Two scoops of *chocolate* with *chocolate* chips and *chocolate* sprinkles and *chocolate* sauce," Amy told the young woman behind the counter at Casey's Ice Cream Parlor.

It was Tuesday afternoon, and Elizabeth and Amy had decided to stop by Casey's on their way home from school.

Amy turned to Elizabeth and giggled. "Can Madame Elizabeth guess what my favorite flavor is?"

Elizabeth put her fingers to her temples and squeezed her eyes shut. "Madame Elizabeth is going to guess . . . *chocolate*!"

Amy opened her mouth in pretend astonishment. "That's amazing!"

Elizabeth stepped up to the counter. "I'd like two scoops of strawberry, with bananas and nuts, please."

She turned and looked around the noisy ice-cream store. "Gosh. It looks like just about the whole school is in here today. There's Jessica." Elizabeth waved at her sister, who was sitting at a large table with some of the other Unicorns.

"Where do you want to sit?" Amy asked. "I don't see any empty tables."

"There are some extra chairs at the Unicorns' table. Let's sit with them."

Amy wrinkled her nose. "Yuck! Do we have to? They act so dumb when they're all together."

"If we don't sit with them, we'll have to stand," Elizabeth pointed out.

"OK," Amy said with a sigh as they paid for their sundaes.

Elizabeth led the way to the Unicorns' table. "Is it OK if we sit with you guys?" she asked.

"Sure," Mandy said, moving her chair over to make room. "We were just talking about the talent show."

"It's going to be fabulous," Ellen Riteman said. "All the posters for the show are going to have my picture on them, since I'm the star." She threw Jessica a patronizing look. "It's too bad you don't have any talent, Jessica."

Jessica looked furious. "I hate to break this to you, Ellen, but neither do—"

"Hey, Jessica!" Randy Mason shouted, interrupting her.

Everyone at the table looked up as Randy came scurrying over.

"What does geek-brain want?" Janet Howell asked under her breath.

Randy was flushed with excitement as he approached the table and sat down. "Guess what, Jessica. I talked to my uncle about you and Elizabeth. And he says he's really interested. He might even want to interview you on camera for his film."

"What!" the Unicorns all exclaimed.

"What film?" Tamara asked.

"Why would Randy's uncle want to interview *you*?" Ellen demanded.

"Well," Jessica began. "I told Randy that Elizabeth and I might be . . ." she threw a nervous glance at Elizabeth, "just a little bit psychic."

"A little bit!" Randy said. "When I told my uncle what you told me, he flipped. He said that it fits in with all the psychic stories he's ever heard about twins. He's been looking for some twins to interview for months."

Elizabeth raised her eyebrows in Jessica's direction, and Jessica blushed and looked away. Elizabeth heard that little warning bell in her brain that meant that Jessica was about to get them both involved in something they'd regret. But before she could ask any questions, the other girls had jumped in.

"What kind of a film is it?" Tamara asked.

"Who is your uncle?" Janet demanded.

"My uncle is a documentary filmmaker," Randy

answered proudly. "He's working on a film about people with psychic powers, and he might want to include an interview with Elizabeth and Jessica in it."

There was an excited scream from almost every Unicorn.

But Elizabeth sat there with her heart sinking. *Here we go again,* she thought. Jessica's outrageous lies and bragging seemed to get them into one scrape after another.

Well, not this time, Elizabeth decided. She didn't know what Jessica had told Randy, but whatever it was, it had to have been totally exaggerated. Two people deciding to eat the same breakfast cereal, or choosing the same topic for a paper, weren't good enough examples of psychic phenomena to bring a Los Angeles filmmaker running down to interview them.

Elizabeth took a deep breath and opened her mouth to protest—but before she could say a word, she saw Jessica throw her a pleading glance. She looked so desperate that Elizabeth shut her mouth with a snap. It wasn't fair to make Jessica look bad in front of her friends. She'd wait till they were in private.

"Don't you think you're all getting a little carried away?" Janet said in a patronizing voice. "Jessica and Elizabeth aren't psychic. That's ridiculous."

Mandy Miller took a bite of her brownie and chewed thoughtfully. "I've read that a lot of the time, twins are more psychic than other kinds of siblings. Like if one of them is in trouble, or something like that, the other one senses it."

"That's right," Randy said, nodding. "That's what my uncle said. And it sure fits in with the story that Jessica told me."

Ah ha, Elizabeth thought. *I was right. Jessica did make up a story.* Elizabeth tried to catch Jessica's eye again. If only there were some way to get them out of this without embarrassing Jessica.

"Well, call me cynical, but I want to see some proof," Janet said.

"Yeah," Ellen added nastily.

Every pair of eyes turned toward Elizabeth and Jessica.

"Could you do something psychic now?" Mandy asked.

Elizabeth glared at Jessica. Jessica shrugged. "We can try," she said.

Randy handed a napkin and a pen to Elizabeth. "Let's start with something easy. Elizabeth, you pick a number between one and one thousand and write it on this napkin. Let's see if Jessica can tell us what number you wrote down."

"Sounds good to me," Janet said, pulling her chair in closer.

Elizabeth felt her heart plummet again. There was no way out of this. Poor Jessica was going to totally embarrass herself.

Elizabeth wrote down the first number that

popped into her head. "OK," she said, turning to Jessica.

Jessica frowned for a moment and chewed her lip. Finally she blew out her breath. "Three hundred and twenty-eight," she said with conviction.

Elizabeth felt her heart jump. Wordlessly, she held up the napkin.

"Three hundred and twenty-eight!" Mandy Miller squealed.

Randy blinked in surprise. "Wow!"

Janet Howell looked taken aback.

Elizabeth swallowed nervously. It was a coincidence. Just another coincidence.

"Do something else," Randy urged. "Jessica, you start it this time. Think of a . . . umm . . . president of the United States!"

Jessica picked up the pen and another napkin and wrote something very quickly. Then she turned it over.

"What did Jessica write, Elizabeth?" Randy asked.

Suddenly, a picture of George Washington popped into Elizabeth's head. "George Washington?" she said with a nervous laugh.

Jessica's eyes grew round and she looked almost frightened. She turned her napkin over. "GEORGE WASHINGTON" was written in big block letters.

Everyone at the table gasped.

"This is starting to scare me," Amy Sutton said quietly.

"Don't be scared," Randy said eagerly. "It's just psychic phenomena. It's fascinating."

But Elizabeth realized her hands were shaking. "I don't want to do it anymore," she said. Amy was right. This *was* getting scary.

"It's some kind of trick!" Ellen said knowingly. "It's definitely a trick. I just can't figure out how they're doing it."

"It can't be a trick," Randy argued. "We're all watching, and they didn't know what questions I was going to ask."

"How do we know *you're* not in on the trick?" Janet demanded.

Randy nodded. "Good point. Why don't you ask them a question?"

Janet turned to Jessica. "Write down the name of an article of clothing—and write down a color, too."

"OK," Jessica agreed happily. She quickly wrote two words on a napkin and handed it to Janet.

"OK, Elizabeth," Janet said. "Tell us what Jessica wrote down."

Elizabeth swallowed nervously. The picture of a tie popped into her head. And for some reason, it made her think of the color black. "A tie," she said in a hoarse whisper.

Janet's eyes widened.

"And the color black," Elizabeth added.

Slowly, Janet turned the napkin and held it up so everyone could see. "TIE" and "BLACK" were written in bold letters.

There was a stunned silence as everybody at the table stared at the twins in awe.

Elizabeth felt just as amazed as the rest of the group. And from the look on Jessica's white face, she guessed Jessica felt the same way.

But it didn't take her sister long to rally. After a moment Jessica's face broke into a broad grin. "See?" she said, tapping her finger against her temple. "Psychic!"

"Concentrate!" Jessica urged her sister. "Concentrate!" She pressed her fingertips against her temples.

Elizabeth squeezed her eyes shut and pressed her fingers against her temples too.

It was Wednesday morning and the girls were sitting at the breakfast table, trying as hard as they could to send each other psychic messages.

"I'm concentrating as hard as I can, but you must not be getting my message," Elizabeth said finally.

Jessica pressed her fingertips even harder against her temples, but all she could think about was Randy's uncle the filmmaker, and how incredibly thrilling it would be to be interviewed in a documentary film.

Elizabeth opened her eyes. "It's not working," she said glumly. "I've been mentally asking you to pass me the jelly for ten minutes now, and you haven't done it."

Jessica pushed the jelly in Elizabeth's direction. "I've got a lot on my mind," she said. "Maybe this psychic stuff is like the telephone. You're just getting a psychic busy signal."

"Or maybe we're not really psychic," Elizabeth responded.

"Don't say that!" Jessica said. "We have to be psychic. We just have to be. Look at what happened at Casey's yesterday. How else can you explain that?"

Elizabeth shrugged. "It *was* pretty spooky."

Jessica poured herself another bowl of Corny-O's. "I can't wait to be in Randy's uncle's movie. Just think how neat it'll be."

Jessica had hardly been able to sleep the night before, she was so excited. The Unicorns were amazed by her psychic ability. And if she got to be in a movie because of it, she'd really have something to brag about.

Ellen Riteman might be the star of the talent show, but that didn't even begin to compare with being in a real movie.

"Jessica," Elizabeth said. "I've been meaning to ask you something. What, exactly, did you tell Randy that made him tell his uncle about us?"

Jessica felt her cheeks get hot. Elizabeth could be a real stickler for the truth. In fact, Jessica wouldn't even put it past her to tell Randy that the story about the basement being flooded was a big lie. If she knew about it, anyway.

"Oh," Jessica said breezily. "I just told him about the Corny-O's and the French Revolution."

"And that made Randy's uncle want to interview us?"

Jessica looked down at her cereal bowl, determined to avoid Elizabeth's searching gaze.

"Come on, Jess, I know you told him more than that."

Jessica examined her fingernails. The problem with Elizabeth was that she had a lie detector in her brain. "I told him about that time, years ago, when Mom and Dad couldn't find you anywhere. I finally told them to look in the basement. And that's where you were. How could I have known you were locked in the basement if I wasn't psychic?"

Elizabeth scowled at her sister. "Jessica! You knew I was in the basement because you were the one who locked me in!"

Jessica looked surprised. "Are you sure?"

"Believe me," Elizabeth said. "I'll never forget it."

Jessica grinned. "I guess I forgot that part. But it still doesn't change the fact that we're psychic now."

"Maybe not," Elizabeth muttered. "But for someone who claims to be psychic, you have a terrible memory."

"Lucky guesses!" Amy exclaimed to Elizabeth on their way to social-studies class that morning. "You've got to be kidding."

"No," Elizabeth said with a worried frown. "I'm

serious. We haven't been able to do one psychic thing since yesterday. We tried really hard this morning, but we couldn't read each other's minds at all. I'm beginning to think we might not really be psychic."

"Maybe your minds were too sleepy," Amy suggested. "Or maybe psychic ability is something that comes and goes. Or maybe . . ."

"Hold it," Elizabeth said with a laugh. "You sound like Jessica. I know why she's so determined to believe we're psychic—she wants to be in Randy's uncle's movie. But I can't figure out why you are."

"I just think it's neat, that's all. And so do lots of other people. It seems like everybody's been talking about it. It really sets Sweet Valley Middle School apart, to have a pair of psychics in residence. There might even be a *Sixers* profile in this."

Elizabeth and Amy both laughed and turned the corner into their social-studies classroom. Elizabeth stopped suddenly in the doorway.

Bruce Patman and Rick Hunter, two seventh-grade boys, were sitting at the front of the room with towels wrapped around their heads like turbans.

As soon as they saw Elizabeth, Rick put his fingertips to his temples. "Silence. Silence. Swami Rick is getting a psychic reading. There's something in the room that rhymes with baloney."

Just then, Jessica came hurrying into the classroom.

Bruce Patman put his fingertips to his temples. "Swami Bruce is getting a psychic reading too. My amazing mental powers tell me there are *two* things in the room that rhyme with baloney."

Rick looked at Bruce with wide eyes. "Gee, I wonder what the message means."

Bruce rubbed his chin thoughtfully. "I wonder if the message means—*phonies!*"

"Ha ha!" Amy said sourly. "Very funny. But if you two had been in Casey's yesterday, you wouldn't be so quick to laugh."

Bruce pulled the towel from his head. "Oh, right," he said sarcastically. "I can't believe the whole school is all excited just because Jessica and Elizabeth pulled off some kind of smoke and mirrors trick."

"It wasn't a trick," Jessica said angrily. "Was it, Elizabeth?"

Elizabeth wet her lips nervously. It hadn't been a trick. But on the other hand, they hadn't been able to do anything psychic since yesterday.

"If it's not a trick," Rick challenged, "how about another demonstration?"

"Yeah," Bruce added. "If you two are psychic, prove it."

Elizabeth's heart sank.

"You're on," Jessica said confidently.

Rick and Bruce looked at each other.

Oh, well, Elizabeth thought. *Maybe it's better this way. I'd rather us make fools of ourselves now, in front of Bruce Patman and Rick Hunter, than later in front of a real filmmaker.*

Amy handed Elizabeth and Jessica each a sheet of paper out of her notebook. "OK. Jessica, you think up a number. Elizabeth, see if you can read Jessica's mind and write the number down."

"Hold it!" Rick said. "That's too easy. Think of *two* numbers."

Jessica squeezed her eyes shut and Elizabeth closed hers too. Oddly enough, two numbers popped into Elizabeth's head. She opened her eyes and wrote them on the paper. Then she handed the paper to Bruce. Rick and Amy both peered at the paper over Bruce's shoulder.

Jessica opened her eyes and stared at Elizabeth for a moment. "Fifteen and twenty-eight," she said confidently.

Elizabeth felt her heart thumping in her chest. Those were the exact two numbers she had written on the page.

It was true! They *were* psychic! Even she was convinced of it now.

"Incredible," Rick breathed.

"Amazing!" Bruce agreed.

"Totally awesome!" Amy said with a happy nod.

Four

"I see a tall, dark stranger," Jessica said, frowning over Lila Fowler's palm in the cafeteria on Friday.

Since their demonstration in Casey's and the episode the day before with Bruce Patman and Rick Hunter, Elizabeth and Jessica had become celebrities—and Jessica was loving every minute of it. Most of the kids seemed kind of unclear about what Jessica's powers were, though. She'd already had two requests for love potions, three requests for palm readings, and Denny Jacobson had asked her to read the bumps on his head.

Jessica didn't have any idea how to brew a love potion or read a palm, but the attention was just irresistible, so she was doing her best to live up to her mystical reputation.

"That's it?" Lila demanded. "A tall, dark stranger?

Doesn't that seem sort of clichéd?"

Jessica felt herself getting angry. Lila Fowler was Jessica's best friend, but sometimes she could be really annoying. Lila's father was one of the wealthiest people in Sweet Valley, and he let Lila buy anything she wanted—including the same green silk blouse that Jessica had been saving money to buy for three weeks.

"I see something green, too," Jessica added spitefully. "Something that's going to cause you a lot of trouble."

"Hmmm." Tamara Chase drummed her fingers on the table. "Let's see. Poison ivy is green. Maybe you'd better stay inside for the next few weeks."

"Money is green too," Kimberly Haver offered. "And Lila's got lots of it."

"It's not poison ivy or money," Jessica intoned, putting her fingertips to her head. "I see . . . a green *blouse*."

Lila snatched her palm from Jessica's hand. "Oh, please! You're just making this up because you're still mad that I bought the blouse you wanted. Well, I'm not giving it to you, Jessica. So forget it."

Just then Mandy Miller came over to the table with her tray. As she moved to take the empty seat next to Lila, she stumbled and her tray tipped.

"Look out!" Tamara cried.

But it was too late. Mandy's bowl of lime Jell-O slid off the tray . . .

. . . and landed right on Lila's shoulder.

"Oh," Mandy gasped. "I'm *so* sorry, Lila."

Everyone stared at Lila's blouse in shock.

"Lila's blouse is green now," Tamara finally breathed.

As Jessica watched the green Jell-O drip down the front of Lila's shirt, she couldn't help smiling. Nobody would doubt her psychic abilities now.

"Bury the chicken bones at exactly eight o'clock tonight behind the hedge in your backyard," Jessica told Lloyd Benson as they walked up to her locker. "Then say Leslie's name five times."

"Are you sure that will get her to like me?" Lloyd asked breathlessly.

"Well, there are never any guarantees," Jessica said evasively. "You may have to do it several times. But it can't hurt. And it might help."

"Wow! This is really great. Thanks, Jessica." Lloyd waved and then hurried away to salvage some chicken bones from the school's cafeteria Dumpster.

Just then, Jessica noticed Elizabeth hovering at her elbow, glaring at her. "What do you think you're doing?" Elizabeth demanded as soon as Lloyd was out of earshot.

"Trying to help people with my psychic powers," Jessica replied.

"Well, cut it out," Elizabeth snapped. "This thing is getting out of control. Do you know that Denny

Jacobson actually asked me to read the bumps on his head?"

Jessica giggled. "He asked me too."

"What did you do?"

"I read them."

"*Jessica!* You don't know how to read the bumps on Denny's head. What if you give somebody advice that's wrong?"

Jessica frowned. "All I did was feel his head and advise him to look both ways before he crossed the street."

Elizabeth shook her head and laughed. "Well, I guess that piece of advice couldn't get anybody into trouble."

"Exactly. So would you please relax and quit taking everything so seriously?" Jessica begged. "Being psychic is fun!"

"Jessica! I've asked you to pass the potatoes five times," Steven complained that night at dinner. "Now hand them over."

Mr. Wakefield looked at Steven in surprise. "I didn't hear you ask for the potatoes."

Steven began to laugh. "I was asking mentally— you know, sending a psychic message."

Mr. Wakefield shook his head. "What is going on here? What's this psychic business you all keep talking about?"

"Lizzie and I are psychic!" Jessica said proudly. "We read minds and everything."

"But only each other's minds," Elizabeth said.

"That's not what I hear," Steven said. "I heard Jessica predicted that Lila was going to get a lime slime at lunch—and she did."

"Who told you that?" Jessica asked eagerly.

"Joe Howell told a bunch of us. You guys are actually getting a rep at high school."

Jessica shrieked in excitement. "All right! We're famous!"

Jessica noticed that Elizabeth was smiling a little too.

"Do you guys believe in psychic phenomena?" Steven asked his parents.

"No," Mr. Wakefield said bluntly.

"DAD!" Jessica protested.

"What about you, Mom?" Steven asked.

But Mrs. Wakefield didn't answer. When Jessica looked over at her mother, she saw that she was staring into space with her fork hovering in front of her mouth.

"Mom?" Jessica prompted, nudging her mother's foot under the table.

Mrs. Wakefield looked startled. "Oh!" she said with a laugh. "I'm sorry. What were you asking me?"

Steven made a mysterious whistling noise. "Looks like it runs in the family," he said. "Mom's in a trance."

"I'm not in a trance," she said, smiling. "I just remembered a few more things I need to do before I leave Monday morning for the convention."

"How come you have to go to a convention?" Steven asked. "Aren't those things kind of boring?"

Mrs. Wakefield laughed. "I don't *have* to go. I *want* to go. The annual designers' convention helps me to keep up with the latest trends. It also gives me an opportunity to meet with decorators from all over the country. There's nothing boring about it."

"When will you be back?" Jessica asked.

"I should be back by Friday evening," Mrs. Wakefield responded.

"What time?" Elizabeth asked.

"If you guys are so psychic," Steven asked, "how come you have to ask so many questions?"

"Oh, shut up," Jessica snapped.

Just then the doorbell rang.

"I wonder who that is," Mrs. Wakefield said.

Steven turned to Jessica. "Who is it, Jess?"

"How should I know?" Jessica said.

Ding-dong!

"Something tells me your psychic powers have been greatly exaggerated," Steven teased.

Ding-dong!

"Yeah? Well, something tells me your intelligence has been greatly exaggerated," Jessica retorted.

Mr. Wakefield tapped his water glass with his spoon. "I hate to interrupt. But would you characters quit arguing and one of you get the door?"

Jessica grinned and hopped up from her chair.

*　　*　　*

Lila came barreling through the door first. "Wait till you hear this!"

Hard on her heels came Tamara Chase, Mandy Miller, and Janet Howell. "You're going to die!" Tamara said.

"This is so incredible!" Mandy added.

"What's going on?" Jessica asked, closing the front door.

Tamara took a deep breath. "The talent show committee had a meeting this afternoon. Bruce Patman is a student representative, and he told them about you and Elizabeth, and guess what? They want you to be in the show."

"*All right!*" Jessica squealed.

"Not only that," Janet Howell said, "they want the Psychic Sisters to be the main attraction instead of Ellen."

"Even though Ellen's mom is on the committee?"

Lila nodded. "My dad's on the board of the Children's Hospital. I told him to call her and tell her that you and Elizabeth would be a much better act. Having you guys as the main attraction would generate more publicity for the hospital than having Ellen singing some moldy old opera aria."

"Ellen's going to be really mad," Tamara said.

"That's just too bad," Janet Howell snapped. "Jessica and Elizabeth will be awesome. And that's going to look great for the Unicorns."

Jessica's jaw dropped. It was incredible. It was

like a dream come true. Not only had she impressed the Unicorns, but she was going to be the main attraction at the talent show. People from all over Sweet Valley would know her name. She was going to be famous. Elizabeth's premonition had come true.

"So what do you say, Jessica? Will you do it?" Tamara asked.

"Of course!" Jessica practically shouted.

"Shouldn't you check with Elizabeth?" Mandy asked.

Jessica pressed her fingertips to her temples. "I'm getting a reading into Elizabeth's mind right now. *And she's going to have a mini-coronary*, she thought. "And I know she'll want to do it," she said.

"Good," Janet said, pulling a piece of paper from her purse. "Here's the entry form. I filled it out for you already. All you have to do is sign it."

Janet handed Jessica a pen. Jessica took it, and with a large, round flourish, she signed her name: Madame Jessica Wakefield, Psychic.

"*No.* No, no, and double no!"

"Elizabeth!" Jessica wheedled, sitting down on the foot of her sister's bed on Sunday night.

"Make that a triple no!" Elizabeth added.

"What's the matter with you?" Jessica demanded. "We both wanted to be in the talent show—now here's our big chance. We can show the whole world our psychic powers."

"I don't want to show the whole world my psychic powers," Elizabeth responded. "I think the whole thing is kind of scary."

"We'd be upholding the honor of Sweet Valley Middle School," Jessica argued. "Don't you care about the school's reputation?"

"Of course I care," Elizabeth said quickly.

"And if we win first prize, we'll win a pair of pro soccer tickets for the whole season."

"That would be pretty cool," Elizabeth said slowly.

Jessica smiled. Elizabeth was weakening. It was time for the clincher.

"And it's for a good cause. All the money from the ticket sales goes to the Sweet Valley Children's Hospital. You wouldn't want to let a whole bunch of sick kids down, would you?"

"Of course not!" Elizabeth exclaimed.

Jessica smiled. "And don't forget, it was you who said I was going to be famous."

"That's right—I said *you* were going to be famous. Why do I have to get dragged into it?"

"Because we're twins," Jessica said magnanimously. "And it's share and share alike."

"We *would* be using our powers for good," Elizabeth mused.

"We sure would. The Children's Hospital is about the worthiest cause I can think of."

"OK, OK, Jess," Elizabeth agreed with a smile. "You've got me once again. I'll do it."

"All right!" Jessica shouted, jumping high in the air.

Later that night, Elizabeth watched Mrs. Wakefield rush up and down the upstairs hall carrying three dresses over one arm and the iron in her other hand.

"Mom? Is there anything I can do to help?" Elizabeth asked.

Her mother had been racing around all evening, trying to get ready for her trip the following morning. Mrs. Wakefield's partner was going to pick her up at 5:30 A.M.

"I don't think so, sweetheart. I'm just going to press these dresses and then . . . *oh!*" Mrs. Wakefield stopped and put her hand to her mouth. "Actually, there *is* something you can do for me."

She put the dresses and the iron down on the table in the hall and disappeared into her bedroom for a moment. When she reappeared, she was holding an envelope. "I'm asking you to do this because I know you won't forget." She smiled at Elizabeth. "You've got the best memory in the family."

Elizabeth smiled. It was nice to know that her mother trusted her.

"Do you know where the Regent Hotel is?"

Elizabeth nodded. "It's a few blocks from school. I've gone by it on my bike lots of times."

"Good." Mrs. Wakefield handed the envelope to Elizabeth. "I need you to take this to the banquet manager at the hotel tomorrow after school. It's a confirmation letter and deposit for the Interior Designers' banquet that I'm organizing. He has to have this in order to reserve the room. I promised him he'd have it by tomorrow. Can you do that?"

"Sure," Elizabeth answered, taking the envelope from her mother.

"There's a check in there, so be very careful not to lose it."

"I won't," Elizabeth promised.

"Thank you so much, honey."

"Glad to be of service," Elizabeth replied with a laugh.

"Alice!" Mr. Wakefield called from downstairs. "Telephone! It's about your ride to the airport tomorrow."

Mrs. Wakefield rushed away to answer the call on the upstairs phone, and Elizabeth went into her room.

She took the envelope and zipped it up in one of the side pockets of her book bag. She hardly ever kept anything in that pocket—so she knew it would be safe and not fall out while she was at school.

The door to the bathroom that connected her room with Jessica's opened, and Jessica came twirling in wearing a long purple dress that was left over from an old Halloween costume. On her head, she wore a bright silk scarf wrapped like a turban.

"I found this stuff in one of the trunks in the attic. What do you think, *Madame Elizabeth*?" Jessica asked.

Elizabeth giggled. "I think you're a little over-dressed for bed."

Jessica grinned. "But not for the talent show!"

"Nope. For the talent show you look great," Elizabeth agreed. "But what should I wear?"

"There's another dress like this and a bunch more scarves in the attic," Jessica said eagerly. "Come on, let's go up and look."

This might actually be fun, Elizabeth thought as she hurried up the attic stairs behind Jessica.

Five

Jessica let out an excited shriek. "Look at us!"

Elizabeth looked over to see what had attracted Jessica's attention. Her eyes widened. "My gosh!"

Hanging in the front hall of Sweet Valley Middle School was a huge poster. On it was a drawing of the Wakefield twins. They were sitting across from each other at a table. A crystal ball was between them, and a lightning bolt connected their heads.

"THE SWEET VALLEY MIDDLE SCHOOL TALENT SHOW PRESENTS—THE PSYCHIC SISTERS," the caption said. Underneath it was all the information about the talent show—time, date, and ticket price.

"Like it?" said a voice behind them.

The twins turned and saw Sarah Thomas smiling shyly at them.

"It's fabulous!" Jessica said. "Absolutely, unbe-lievably fantastic! Did you paint it?"

Sarah nodded proudly. "The talent show com-mittee called me over the weekend and asked if I could do it really fast. I finished it last night, and my dad took it to a copy place this morning. By this afternoon, there will be twenty more just like it hanging all over town."

Sarah Thomas was a friend of Elizabeth's and a very talented artist.

"It looks great!" Elizabeth confirmed. "It's just too bad they can't put visual artists in the talent show. You'd definitely win."

"My name will be in the program," Sarah said proudly.

Jessica stepped closer to the poster and frowned. There was something a little odd about one of the twins' pictures. "Which one is me and which one is Elizabeth?" she asked.

Sarah knitted her eyebrows and thought for a minute. Then she pointed to the twin on the left side of the poster. "I guess this one is Elizabeth. The one on the right is you because she's wearing a purple shirt."

"It almost looks like I have Ellen Riteman's nose," Jessica observed. "Hmmm . . . And it looks like I have Ellen Riteman's smile, too."

"Jessica!" Elizabeth scolded. "Don't be so criti-cal. It's a great poster."

"Well, it's true," Jessica protested. She pointed to

the face of the twin on the right side of the poster. "See that? The nose and the mouth look *just like* Ellen Riteman's."

Sarah flushed pink with embarrassment. "You're right. I was hoping nobody would notice. See, when the committee first asked me to do the poster, they told me Ellen Riteman was going to be the star. So I started drawing a picture of Ellen Riteman. But when they called and told me that *you guys* were the stars, I didn't have time to start completely over, so I had to turn Ellen into one of you guys." She laughed. "Sorry about that."

Jessica was proud to be on a poster, but it was a drag to have Ellen's face. "It's too bad Ellen is so much uglier than me," she mumbled. "If I'm going to be on twenty posters all over town, I want to look my best."

"Gee, thanks!" an angry voice said.

All three girls turned and saw Ellen looking at them through narrow eyes.

Oops! Jessica thought.

"I can't believe they would actually replace me with somebody like you!" Ellen said angrily.

"What's that supposed to mean?" Jessica demanded.

"Everybody knows that there's no such thing as psychic power," Ellen sniffed. "You guys are a couple of fakes, and your act is totally phony."

"We are not fakes," Jessica argued. "And our act is not phony."

"Oh, sure," Ellen said sarcastically. "Personally, I think it's pretty awful what you're doing. People are paying money for these tickets. They should get to see real talent."

"Then maybe you should drop out altogether," Jessica shot back.

"Very funny!" Ellen sneered. She stared angrily at the poster and tapped her foot. "I can't wait for the talent show. I can't wait to see you two be totally humiliated!"

"But you're *not* phonies!" Maria Slater said that afternoon. "So what are you worrying about?"

Elizabeth shrugged and sat down on Maria's bed. "It's starting to seem kind of chancy. I mean, we were never psychic before. What if we can't be psychic on the night of the talent show?"

"Don't listen to her," Jessica said impatiently. She sat down next to Elizabeth and tossed her hair over her shoulder. "I'm not worried about our psychic powers at all. We'll be psychic when the time comes. I'm sure of it. What I am a little worried about, though, is our stage presence."

"That's why we came over," Elizabeth explained. "We were sort of hoping you could give us some tips on how to make our act more dramatic."

Maria sighed enviously. "I wish I were going to be in the show."

"Why aren't you?" Jessica asked. "You're the

only person in school with any professional stage experience."

Maria Slater had been a child star in Hollywood before she and her family moved to Sweet Valley. They had left Hollywood because her parents wanted Maria to have a normal childhood filled with friends and school activities, instead of grow-ing up on a movie set.

"That's exactly why I can't be in the show," Maria explained. "I have professional experience, and the talent show is open only to amateurs."

"I guess the talent show committee is afraid you'd steal the show," Jessica said with a grin.

Maria nodded, and her eyes sparkled. "And they're absolutely right. I *would* steal the show if I could. I was a notorious scene-stealer when I was a kid. I was always upstaging my costars if I thought I could get away with it."

Elizabeth frowned. "Didn't they get mad? I mean, it doesn't sound very fair."

"No. But that's show business. And I only did it when I thought a scene was going flat or wasn't working. Then I'd jump in there and do anything I could to get a laugh or make people cry, whether it was in the script or not. Show business isn't about being fair to performers; it's about being fair to the audience and making sure they're entertained."

Elizabeth nodded. "I guess you're right."

"You know, I was once in a TV movie about a psychic," Maria said.

"You're kidding!" Jessica exclaimed.

"No. But the psychic in the movie was a phony. She was using her act to bilk people out of lots of money. I played her granddaughter, who she forces to help her in her schemes. The psychic and the granddaughter have this whole code worked out for relaying information to each other. But they pretend like they're reading people's minds."

"What happened at the end f the movie?" Jessica asked.

"The detective catches her ar the phony psychic gets arrested by the police."

Elizabeth swallowed hard. "Really?" she asked in a hoarse whisper.

Maria noticed Elizabeth's white face. "What's the matter, Elizabeth?"

"I guess I'm just nervous about the show. I'm beginning to wish Jessica and I had never found out we were psychic."

"Stage fright," Maria said knowingly. "And I know just the thing for it."

"You do?" Jessica asked.

Maria nodded. "Get your backpacks and come with me."

"Three ice-cream sundaes, please," Maria told the man behind the counter at Casey's.

"Ice cream! For stage fright?" Elizabeth said with a giggle.

"You bet," Maria said. "Ice cream is great for

stage fright." Her face became very serious. "A fa- mous doctor in London discovered this little- known fact. He was the personal physician to Sarah Bernhardt, a famous actress who had a terri- ble problem with stage fright. The only thing that got her on stage, night after night, was eating an ice-cream sundae before each performance."

"Really?" Jessica breathed.

"No," Maria said with a laugh. "I really just wanted some ice cream, and it was a good way to get you two over here."

Elizabeth laughed. "You and Jessica have a lot in common. Jessica will tell people anything to get them to do what she wants."

"That's not true," Jessica protested.

"No?" Elizabeth teased. "Then how did I get in- volved in this talent show?"

"Ha ha," Jessica said sourly.

"Ha ha, yourself," Elizabeth retorted.

"I had another reason for telling you that," Maria said seriously. "I wanted to illustrate a point. You see, I told you something totally ridiculous. But for a minute there, I made you believe it. That's what stagecraft is all about. What happens on a stage is all illusion. It's the performer's job to make the audience believe it."

The man behind the counter brought out their sundaes.

"Come on," Maria said, picking hers up. "Let's get a table and I'll give you some performing tips."

"First tip," Maria said, when they were settled at a table. "Keep all of your gestures big and dramatic."

"Hmmm . . . like this?" Elizabeth asked. She made a sweeping gesture with her arm, and pressed her fingertips against her forehead.

"Exactly!" Maria said. "Now you try it, Jessica."

Jessica swept her arm around in an even bigger, grander gesture.

"That's great," Maria said approvingly. "Now for tip number two . . ."

Twenty minutes later, Elizabeth was feeling one hundred percent better about the talent show.

Maria had given them tips on how to look taller, how to make eye contact with the audience, and how to humorously ad-lib their way through any mistakes they might make.

"I'm really beginning to look forward to this show," Elizabeth said with a smile. "Maybe even as much as you are, Jess. And you're right: even if we don't get any psychic messages, what's the worst that can happen? We'll put on a good show and entertain the audience. Besides, most of the people in the audience will be our friends. They'll know we did the best we could, even if our best isn't all that great."

Maria nodded. "The best thing you can do," she assured them, "is get out there and have fun. If you guys are having fun, the audience will too."

Elizabeth scraped the last bit of chocolate out of her ice-cream bowl. "You know, I think that business about ice cream curing stage fright might not be so ridiculous after all. I don't feel frightened at all anymore."

"Elizabeth! Jessica!"

The girls looked up and saw Randy Mason hurrying over to them. "Wait till you guys hear this!"

"What's up?" Jessica asked. "Did you hear anything from your uncle?"

"I sure did. I told him about you guys being in the talent show, and guess what?"

"What?"

"He's going to come to the show. He's going to bring a camera and videotape your act for his film."

Jessica closed her eyes and shrieked. "Unbelievable!"

"Fantastic!" Maria shouted.

"Great!" Elizabeth croaked, feeling the color drain from her face.

Maria looked over at Elizabeth and frowned. "What's the matter, Elizabeth? You look really pale."

Elizabeth gulped and held out her bowl. "You'd better get me another ice-cream sundae," she said weakly. "I think I'm having a relapse of stage fright."

Six

◇

"But what if we can't be psychic under pressure?" Elizabeth moaned that evening. She flopped down on Jessica's bed. "What if we freeze up when we see the camera? What if we're like those bird acts they have on late-night TV—the ones who are supposed to talk, but when they get on the show, never make a peep?"

Jessica didn't seem to be listening. She was busily pulling everything out of her closet. "I'm not sure I have enough clothes to be famous," she said, frowning.

She opened a drawer and began counting her sweaters. "I checked *TV Watchers Weekly*. There are fifteen talk shows, and I figure we could be invited to be on all of them. I think we should try to wear something different on each show, don't you?"

"Jessica!" Elizabeth shouted.

"I'm going to have to ask Dad for a bigger allowance," Jessica continued. "Being famous is probably pretty expensive. I'll bet limos cost a lot of money."

"Jessica!" Elizabeth shouted again in frustration.

"What?"

"Would you stop thinking about clothes and TV shows for a minute and think about our act? If we bomb, believe me, nobody's going to ask us to be on any talk shows."

"Would you stop worrying?" Jessica said. "You're going to jinx us if you keep this up. Stop worrying that we'll flop on the big night, and start convincing yourself we'll be fabulous." She turned her palms to the ceiling. "Get yourself psyched to be psychic."

Elizabeth sat up on the bed. "That's not a bad idea," she said. "Getting psyched, I mean. Let's have a practice session. That'll get me psyched."

"Great," Jessica agreed cheerfully. She hopped on the bed and crossed her legs. "Let's start right now."

"No! No, no, no!" Jessica shouted. "I wasn't thinking of a German shepherd. I was thinking of a peony."

"What?" Elizabeth shouted back. "Are you kidding me? A peony? That isn't a kind of dog."

"It isn't?"

"It's a kind of flower."

"Oh," Jessica said.

Elizabeth glared angrily at her sister. "How am I supposed to figure out what kind of dog you're thinking of when you're thinking of a flower?" she demanded.

"Don't yell at me," Jessica said. "It breaks my psychic mood."

Elizabeth groaned and flopped facedown on the bed. "I give up. We've been trying for twenty minutes and neither one of us has been able to read the other's mind. We haven't gotten one thing right."

Jessica frowned. "Don't you dare give up. And don't just lie there. Sit up."

Elizabeth reluctantly sat back up. "Why isn't it working, Jess?"

"Probably because we're too tense," Jessica said. "What we need to do is relax and think positively."

As Elizabeth watched, Jessica closed her eyes, and her face became calm. She pressed her fingertips to her temples and let out a long, low, throaty moan. "I sense negative karma all around me. It's blocking my psychic energy . . . ohhhmmm . . . But I have a vision. A vision of us at the talent show. A vision of us being a big hit. A vision of us being on a talk show. I'm wearing a new purple sweater . . . the one they have in the window at Valley Fashions . . ."

Elizabeth grabbed Jessica's pillow and whacked Jessica on the head with it. "Would you quit thinking about talk shows and keep your mind on the talent show?"

Jessica opened her eyes and grinned. "We'll try it again tomorrow. Don't worry, Lizzie. It'll work. You'll see."

"Blue!"

Elizabeth shook her head. "No."

"Red!"

"Uh-uh."

"Magenta!"

"Nope."

"Concentrate, Elizabeth. Concentrate!"

"I'm concentrating as hard as I can," Elizabeth wailed. "I'm concentrating so hard, my head hurts."

Jessica let out an impatient sigh. "Then *don't* concentrate so hard. Because my head is starting to hurt too." She brightened. "See! We *are* psychic. We even get each other's headaches."

Elizabeth moaned and sat back in her chair. "It's Tuesday. We're going to have to be more psychic than this by Friday. I think the audience is going to want to see more than the two of us up onstage getting a headache."

Wednesday afternoon, Jessica hurried around a corner and almost collided with Janet Howell, Ellen Riteman, and Denny Jacobson.

"Yeow!" Janet cried, dropping her books.

"Watch it!" Ellen shouted.

"Sorry," Jessica said, quickly bending down to help Janet retrieve her books.

"Well!" Ellen said huffily. "If you're so psychic, how come you didn't know we were coming around the corner?"

Jessica pursed her lips angrily. "Because most of the time, I'm psychic only with Elizabeth. If it had been Elizabeth coming around the corner, I probably would have sensed it."

"But sometimes you're psychic about other people, too," Denny argued. "That was really good advice you gave me the other day."

Jessica had to stop and think. She'd given so much advice to people, she couldn't remember whom she had told what. "What did I advise you to do?" she asked.

"You told me to be sure to look both ways before I crossed the street," Denny answered.

"Big deal," Ellen said, giving Jessica a withering stare. "That's just common sense. You don't have to be psychic to know that it's a good idea to look both ways before you cross the street."

"Yeah! But I live on a one-way street. Usually, I just look one way before I cross it. But yesterday, I looked both ways. And it was a good thing I did, because there was a car coming down the street the wrong way. If I hadn't looked both ways, I might have been hit."

Jessica's heart soared. She *was* psychic. She had to be. Denny's story confirmed it.

Denny gave her a grateful smile. "Thanks again for the good advice," he said. He gave the girls a wave. "I've got to get to class. See you guys later."

"I don't care what he says. *I* still say it's all a bunch of baloney," Ellen said as Denny wandered away. "And on Friday night, everybody is going to know that Jessica and Elizabeth are phonies."

She stepped closer to Jessica and glared at her through narrow eyes. "Just remember. When you get up there on that stage Friday night, you're representing the Unicorns. If you blow it, we all look bad. And if you make the Unicorns look bad, I'll see to it that you get voted out of the club—*permanently*."

"Look who's talking," Jessica retorted angrily. "If anybody is going to make us look bad, it'll be you and your horrible singing."

"Hah!" Ellen barked. Then she shoved her books under her arm and stalked away with her nose in the air.

"Don't pay any attention to Ellen," Janet said quickly. "She's just mad because she's not the star of the show anymore. The rest of us are very proud of you."

Jessica chewed nervously on her fingernail. "I know," she said in a worried voice. "But what if, for some strange reason, Elizabeth and I *weren't* psychic on the big night? The Unicorns wouldn't really vote to throw me out, would they?"

Janet frowned thoughtfully. "Well, that *would*

make us all look pretty bad. But why are you worrying about that? You and Elizabeth are definitely psychic, *aren't* you?"

"Y—yes," Jessica admitted. "But it's not always easy to be psychic on demand."

Janet's eyebrows arched dangerously. "Well, I hope for your sake that you and Elizabeth *are* psychic on the big night. Because if you make a fool out of yourself, you make fools out of all of us. And if you make fools out of all of us . . . well, let's just say it won't be pretty."

"Hey! Wakefield! Wait!"

Steven stopped and saw Joe Howell jogging toward him. "What's up?" Steven asked.

"Are you going to this talent show on Friday?" Joe asked.

"The middle-school thing? The one my sisters are in?" Steven rolled his eyes. "Why would I want to do that?"

Joe shrugged. "Actually, a bunch of us are going. Rumors have been floating around about your sisters. Everybody's dying to see what they can do."

"Really?" Steven said in suprise.

"Yeah. It could be really cool." Joe hoisted his backpack over his shoulder. "A lot of people are going out of their way to check them out. I just hope they're not making all this up."

Steven nodded grimly. "I hope not too."

*　　　*　　　*

"Hey!" Elizabeth protested as Jessica grabbed the mystery she was reading from her hands and threw it behind the sofa. "What are you doing?"

"What am *I* doing?" Jessica yelled, waving her arms in the air. "What are *you* doing reading a book when we've got work to do?" Jessica threw Elizabeth's backpack in the corner. "Get up. Get up. Don't just sit there!" she shouted.

"What's going on? Why are you in such a panic all of a sudden?" Elizabeth asked, staring at her twin in amazement.

Jessica ran into the kitchen, then reappeared a few seconds later with a broom, a mop, and a yardstick. "Help me make a pyramid."

Elizabeth frowned in confusion. "Why do you want to make a pyramid?"

"You'll see," Jessica said as she carefully propped up the broom, the mop, and the yardstick. "There!" she said with satisfaction.

"That's a pyramid?" Elizabeth asked doubtfully.

"Sure. Now, we're going to sit under the pyramid, and it's going to strengthen our psychic powers."

"How?"

"I don't know how. It just will. Haven't you ever heard of pyramid power?"

"Uh, I guess. But I'm not sure they meant a pyramid made out of a broom, a mop, and a yardstick."

"*Cut out that negative thinking!*" Jessica shouted.

"Would you quit yelling and screaming and tell me what's going on?" Elizabeth demanded.

"They're going to throw me out of the Unicorns if our act bombs," Jessica explained.

"You're kidding!"

Jessica shook her head. "That's when it hit me. We really *might* bomb. And if we do, it'll be awful. That's why we've got to practice, practice, practice. Now quit arguing and come get under this pyramid."

"I'm not arguing!" Elizabeth insisted as she watched her sister lower her head and crawl under the handle of the broom.

"Come on!" Jessica said impatiently.

Elizabeth sighed and crawled underneath it too. "Okay. But I feel silly."

Jessica crossed her legs and closed her eyes. "Ahhh," she said, her face assuming a calm expression.

"Can you feel your psychic powers coming back?" Elizabeth asked hopefully.

Jessica opened her eyes. "No, it just feels good to get off my feet. I ran all the way home."

"Oh." Elizabeth looked around, waiting for something to happen. She closed her eyes. Did she feel any different? Nope. She put her hands to her temples, as Jessica always did, and tried to concentrate. She'd send Jessica a psychic message and see if Jessica responded. She'd send her a message that said her hair was sticking out on one side. Jessica was always very concerned about her appearance. She'd want to know that her hair was sticking out funny.

Elizabeth concentrated as hard as she could. *Jessica, your hair is sticking out on one side. Your hair is sticking out on one side. Your hair is sticking out on one side.*

Slam!

Elizabeth and Jessica both jumped at the sound of the front door. Elizabeth's elbow jostled the broom handle, and the pyramid came tumbling down.

"Ouch!" Jessica yelped as the yardstick bounced off of her head.

Elizabeth looked up and saw Steven standing in the doorway with his hands on his hips.

"OK, you two," he said in an angry voice. "It's one thing if you guys want to make fools out of yourselves, but now you're dragging me into it too. A bunch of my friends are going to see you at the talent show, so your act better not bomb."

"Don't worry. Our act is not going to bomb!" Jessica insisted.

Elizabeth sighed. She wished she felt as confident as Jessica.

Jessica began to rebuild the pyramid. "Our act will *not* bomb!" she said in a firm voice. "We *are* psychic!" she said in an even firmer voice. "We are going to be a *big* hit!"

"I hope so," Steven said grimly. "Because if

not . . . Well . . . Let's just say it won't be pretty."

Jessica shook her head as she watched Steven disappear up the stairs. "Why do people keep *saying* that?"

Elizabeth nervously wet her lips. "Jessica," she said softly. "Maybe we should think about dropping out of the talent show. We could say that our psychic powers were getting a little rusty, and . . ."

Elizabeth broke off as the phone began to ring.

"Jessica!" Steven shouted a moment later. "It's Lila."

Jessica ran to the phone in the hallway.

Elizabeth sat in the middle of the floor and waited, listening to the sound of Jessica's muffled voice coming from the hallway. She chewed her fingernail impatiently.

As soon as Jessica came back, Elizabeth decided, she was going to talk her into dropping out of the talent show. Whatever psychic powers they had seemed to have had disappeared, and it was pretty silly to think they would suddenly come back on the night of the talent show. And besides, Steven was right. They didn't have any right to make *him* look bad too.

"Guess what?" Jessica said, appearing in the doorway with a determined expression on her face. "Lila's dad wants to throw a big party for us after the talent show on Friday night. He's going to invite everybody in the show, all the board members from the Children's Hospital, and even some people from the local TV news programs."

"Oh, nooo!" Elizabeth wailed. "Jessica! This is getting way out of hand. Call her back and tell her to cancel it. Then let's call the school and say we can't go on."

Jessica put her hands on her hips, her eyes flashing angrily. "Oh, yes we *can* go on. And we will. Nobody's ever thrown a big party like this in my honor before. And if you think I'm going to back out now, you're wrong."

"But, Jessica . . ."

Jessica began to pace. "We are psychic! I just know it. There's no way we could have done all the stuff we did unless we were psychic."

That was true, Elizabeth reflected. No matter how hard she tried to convince herself that they had just made a series of lucky guesses, she couldn't just write it off as luck.

She looked up at Jessica, and then . . . miraculously . . . Jessica's hand lifted *and she smoothed her hair*!

"Jessica!" Elizabeth shouted. "You just smoothed your hair."

"So?"

"So . . . your hair was sticking out funny. That's the message I've been sending you."

Jessica squealed happily. "See? All right!"

Elizabeth quickly began to reassemble the pyramid. Maybe they were clutching at straws here, but it was all they had. "Let's get back to work. Maybe there is something to this pyramid business after all."

Seven

Elizabeth had just pulled on her nightgown and crawled under the covers when she heard a soft knock on the door. "Come in," she called out.

Mr. Wakefield stuck his head in the door. "Mom called while you were in the bathtub," he said. "She's going to take an earlier plane back on Friday so she can be at the talent show."

Elizabeth smiled, but felt a little flutter in her stomach. "That's great. Seeing you and Mom in the audience is definitely going to help build our confidence."

Mr. Wakefield chuckled. "We're always glad to be of service. Good night, honey."

He shut the door, and Elizabeth turned out her light and lay down. She closed her eyes and felt herself drifting off to sleep . . . until suddenly her eyelids flew open in horror.

Glad to be of service! she heard her father's voice echo.

She'd said the same thing to her mother—*when she had promised to take the letter and the check to the Regent Hotel!*

Elizabeth's heart gave a hard knock against her ribs and she sat straight up in bed. In all the excitement and anxiety over the talent show, she'd completely forgotten that she had promised to take the letter.

She let out a sigh. She'd call the banquet manager at the hotel first thing in the morning.

Elizabeth lay back down and closed her eyes. She felt terrible. It was going to be hard to fall asleep now. Her brain was whirling . . . thinking about the letter, and the check, and the talent show, and the . . . zzzzzzz.

"Where are the waiters?" Mrs. Wakefield asked.

"Where is the band?" Mr. Wakefield asked.

"Where is the food!" shouted the huge roomful of people, all dressed up in evening gowns and tuxedos.

Elizabeth stood with her family in the doorway of the big banquet room and stared around her in horror.

"I don't understand," her mother wailed. "I wrote a letter and sent a check. I gave it to Elizabeth to deliver."

A man wearing old-fashioned clothes and a

tricorner hat stepped forward. Under the hat was a white wig. "I never received the letter, or the check," he said gravely. "That's why I didn't hire the waiters, book the band, or prepare any food."

"Why! It's George Washington!" Mr. Wakefield exclaimed. "The first president of the United States."

George Washington bowed. "Former president," he corrected. "Now I'm the banquet manager of the Regent Hotel. I was expecting this group on the twenty-eighth or the fifteenth. But they all showed up this evening, and we don't have any food to serve them."

"Booooo!" the crowed yelled.

"Ohhh!" Elizabeth gasped. "It's all my fault. I forgot to deliver the letter."

"Maybe we could send out for pizzas," Mr. Wakefield suggested. "How many people are there?"

"I counted three hundred and twenty-eight," George Washington answered.

"No pizza!" the crowed shouted.

"I didn't put on black tie to eat pizza!" a man shouted angrily.

Ellen Riteman was sitting at a nearby table. "I knew the Wakefields were big nothings," she said with a sneer. "Elizabeth isn't psychic. She doesn't even have a good memory. She and Jessica are big phonies. Boooooo!"

"Boooooo!" the room echoed.

Mrs. Wakefield's hands flew to her face. "This is

horrible. This is awful. I'll never live it down. This whole dinner was my responsibility, and it's a disaster."

"We'll have to leave the country," Mr. Wakefield cried.

"I'll have to leave school," Steven said.

"They'll throw me out of the Unicorns," Jessica moaned.

"Elizabeth!" Mrs. Wakefield wailed. "How could you do this to us?"

Elizabeth's eyes flew open and she sat up in bed, her heart pounding. "What a horrible dream!" she gasped. "What a horrible and strange dream."

She quickly reached over and turned on the bedside light, trying to put the nightmare in some order. Suddenly, her mouth felt very dry. The images in her dream seemed awfully familiar. Three hundred and twenty-eight people. George Washington. Black tie!

They were all the things that she and Jessica had guessed when reading each other's minds. Very strange. And somehow, they were connected with her mother's banquet.

"No," she whispered, her eyes growing large and round as a terrible thought occurred to her. "Oh no."

She threw back the covers and raced over to her desk. Furiously, she rooted through her backpack until she found the letter her mother had given her. It wasn't sealed, so Elizabeth didn't worry about opening it. She quickly pulled out the letter and her eyes raced over it.

> Dear Mr. Peters:
> This letter is to confirm our telephone conversation of last Saturday morning. The California Interior Designers' Association would like to reserve the George Washington Room of the Regent Hotel for their annual black-tie dinner to be held on the 28th of next month. We expect that there will be 328 people attending. I have enclosed a check for the deposit.
>
> Sincerely,
Alice Wakefield
>
> P.S. As discussed, if the 15th does become available, please let me know as soon as possible.

Elizabeth took the letter and flew through the bathroom that connected her room and Jessica's.

"W–what!" Jessica shrieked in alarm as Elizabeth jumped onto her bed.

Elizabeth grabbed her arm and shook it. "Wake up, Jessica. Wake up."

"I'm awake. I'm awake," Jessica said, struggling up to a sitting position. "What's wrong? What's going on?"

Elizabeth reached over and turned on Jessica's

bedside lamp. Then she shoved the letter in Jessica's hands. "Read that!"

Jessica rubbed her eyes and read groggily. Then she shrugged. "So?"

"Don't you see?" Elizabeth demanded. "Three hundred and twenty-eight people. Black tie. The George Washington Room."

Jessica stared back at her grumpily. "It's four o'clock in the morning, Elizabeth. I don't know what you're jabbering about, but I'd really rather talk about it in the morning."

She started to lie down, but Elizabeth grabbed the shoulder of her nightgown and pulled her back up. "Don't go to sleep! This is important. Now I see why we zeroed in on so many of the same things, the same images. We must have overheard Mom's conversation with the banquet manager when we were asleep in the living room that Saturday morning. Our conscious minds were asleep. But our unconscious minds were listening to the whole thing."

Jessica frowned in confusion and Elizabeth shook the letter. "It's all there, Jessica. George Washington. The numbers—three hundred and twenty-eight, fifteen, and twenty-eight. Black tie. All the things we thought we were reading from each other's minds."

"Oh, no!" Jessica breathed.

"Oh, yes!" Elizabeth wailed.

"We're not psychic," Jessica gasped.

"We never were!"

"But what about all the other stuff? The Corny-O's and the French Revolution? The lime slime and all that?"

"Those were just coincidences," Elizabeth moaned. "And if they weren't, there's got to be some logical explanation that we just don't know about. Oh, Jessica! *What* are we going to do?"

Jessica's eyes narrowed. "I don't know," she whispered. "But I'll think of something. I always do."

Elizabeth let out a deep breath. "I know. That's what's worrying me."

"Hello," Elizabeth said nervously into the phone the next morning. "May I speak to Mr. Peters?"

"This is Mr. Peters," a friendly voice answered. "May I help you?"

"This is Mrs. Wakefield's daughter, Elizabeth. My mom is out of town, and I was supposed to bring you a letter and a check for the designers' banquet. I'm really sorry, but I forgot to bring it to you on Monday. Is it too late?"

"It's not too late," Mr. Peters replied in a reassuring tone. "Your mother is a lovely lady and we appreciate her business. I'm holding the room for her, but I do need to get the confirmation letter and deposit soon."

Elizabeth heaved a sigh of relief. "May I bring it over after school today?"

"Actually, I'm going to be out of my office all afternoon today and most of tomorrow. It would be better for me if you could bring it by late tomorrow afternoon, say around five."

Elizabeth did some quick calculating. If she dropped the letter off at five, that would give her plenty of time to get back to school for the talent show, which started at seven. Her stomach clenched at the thought of the talent show.

"Five o'clock will be fine," she said in a weak voice.

"Good," Mr. Peters said. "I'll see you then."

Eight

◇

Elizabeth breathed a big sigh of relief as she shoved her books into her locker that afternoon. At least school was over. It had felt like the longest day of her life. She was so worried and jittery that she hadn't been able to concentrate in class. And every time anyone mentioned the talent show, the knot in her stomach tightened.

Suddenly she felt a hand tugging her sleeve. She turned and saw her sister. "Come on," Jessica hissed, a suspicious gleam in her eye.

Elizabeth's mental warning bell went off. That gleam meant Jessica had come up with a plan. And she knew too well that any plan of Jessica's should be approached with extreme caution. "What's up?" Elizabeth asked warily.

Jessica smiled. "I think I've solved our problem. Follow me."

Elizabeth swallowed hard and followed Jessica down the hall and into an empty classroom. "Maria!" she exclaimed.

Maria sat on a desk holding a thick folder. "Hi!" she said with a smile.

Elizabeth's eyes darted back and forth between Jessica and Maria. "What's going on here?"

"I told her everything," Jessica said.

Maria threw back her head and laughed. "Boy. What a story. And I thought *Hollywood* was full of drama."

Elizabeth frowned. "I'm glad somebody's enjoying this."

Maria laughed again. "Don't worry. I think I can help you guys with your problem."

"You're an actress, not a psychic," Elizabeth pointed out.

"I know. But show biz is show biz." She held up the folder again. "Remember that movie I told you about? The one about the phony psychic?"

Elizabeth swallowed hard. "The one who got arrested?"

Maria nodded. "Well, this is the script from that movie. There's a whole system in here for sending signals to each other by wiggling your ears and blinking and stuff like that. I can teach it to you guys."

"No way!" Elizabeth said in a firm voice. "I don't want to do anything dishonest. We're supposed to be for-real psychics, not phonies. People are paying money to see us."

"Elizabeth!" Jessica protested. "Maria's right. It's show biz. People pay money to see magicians, too, and they don't *really* believe the magicians are sawing people in half or making rabbits appear out of thin air."

"I guess," Elizabeth said slowly. "But we're not supposed to be magicians; we're supposed to be psychics. I'm sorry," she said finally. "I just don't think it's right."

Jessica sat down heavily in a chair. "Then we're goners," she wailed. "Our lives are ruined. The Unicorns are going to throw me out of the club. Steven will be the laughingstock of Sweet Valley High. And Mom and Dad will probably ground us both for the rest of our lives."

Elizabeth felt awful. Jessica's voice was quavering and she looked pale. "I'm sorry," Elizabeth said again.

Jessica shook her head. "Don't worry about me," she said in a low voice. "I'll be . . ." But Jessica didn't finish her sentence. Her hands covered her eyes and her shoulders began to shake.

"Jessica!" Elizabeth cried, hurrying to Jessica's side. "Please don't cry. Please!"

"I can't . . . can't . . . h–h–help it," Jessica wept in a shuddery voice.

"It'll be OK, Jess," Maria said soothingly, patting Jessica on the back.

Elizabeth's heart plummeted into her shoes. She really felt terrible. She just hated to make her sister cry. "Oh, all right!" she practically shouted. "I'll do it. I'll do it. Just please don't cry anymore."

"You'll really do it?" Jessica sniffled.

"Yes," Elizabeth said with a sigh.

Immediately, Jessica lifted her face. Her cheeks were dry and there were no signs of tears in her eyes. She grinned. "Great!"

Elizabeth put her hands angrily on her hips. "*Jessica!* You big faker!"

"Actress!" Jessica corrected. She darted a smile at Maria. "Thanks for the acting lesson. Now, if you're as good at teaching us to use that code as you were at teaching me to pretend to cry, we're sure to be a big hit."

Maria laughed and opened the script. "OK, you guys, pay attention, because we've got a lot of ground to cover."

Jessica blinked once, paused, and then scratched her nose twice. She paused again. Then, almost imperceptibly, she bit her lower lip.

"Okaayyy," Elizabeth said with a frown of concentration. "A blink stands for an R." She consulted the crib sheet in her hand. "A nose scratch stands for a B. And, let's see, a lower-lip bite is a T."

"She's thinking of an animal," Maria reminded Elizabeth.

Elizabeth nodded. "Right. So, let's see. R, blank,

B, B, blank . . . T . . . You're thinking of a rabbit," Elizabeth guessed.

Jessica clapped her hands. "Right!"

Elizabeth smiled. "Great. We're batting a thousand. I just hope we can remember the code."

"It's really simple," Maria said quickly. "All you have to do is memorize 21 gestures that correspond with consonants. Once you have the consonants, it's just a simple word puzzle to fill in the right vowel and figure out the word."

"What if it takes us a while to figure out the word?" Elizabeth asked with a worried frown.

"Don't worry about that," Maria said. "If you look like you're stumped for a few moments, it just heightens the suspense."

Elizabeth looked down again at the list of gestures and consonants. "I'm going to have to spend some time studying this."

"I've already got it memorized," Jessica said proudly.

Elizabeth laughed. "I know. How come you can memorize something like this in no time at all, but you can't memorize anything for a test?"

Jessica grinned. "Because getting an A on a history test won't get me into a movie."

Elizabeth and Maria laughed.

"OK, now tell me exactly how you're going to do your act," Maria said.

"Jessica and I will be up onstage," Elizabeth explained. "A third person will pick four or five people out of the audience and have them come up to the edge of the stage. Those people will write down a word on an index card. Each person will write down a kind of vegetable, or the name of a state, or something like that. Then our assistant will give me or Jessica the card, and we'll send each other 'psychic communications' and guess what's written on each other's cards."

Maria nodded approvingly. "Sounds like a good plan. Who are you going to use as your assistant?"

"We thought we'd ask one of the teachers," Elizabeth said. "Unless you have a better idea."

"How about me?" Maria suggested.

"That would be fantastic!" Jessica cried.

"But I thought you said you couldn't be in the show," Elizabeth said.

Maria smiled slyly. "I can't *perform*, but I *can* assist. And I'll do anything to get in Randy's uncle's film."

Elizabeth laughed. "I was right. You and Jessica are just alike."

"Excuse me, girls," said a voice in the doorway. "I've got to lock up now."

The girls looked up and saw Mr. Jackson, the janitor, standing in the door, smiling at them.

Elizabeth stood up. "Sure thing, Mr. Jackson. We were just leaving."

"What are you girls doing here so late? Studying for a big exam?" he asked.

"Well, we *are* studying, but not for an exam,"

Jessica said with a grin at Elizabeth and Maria.

"Well, don't work too hard." Mr. Jackson disappeared down the hallway, rattling his big bunch of keys.

Maria stood and slung her backpack over her shoulder. "Don't worry, guys. As long as you memorize the code and stick to questions that can be answered in one word, you'll be a smash." She gave them an encouraging smile. "Break a leg," she said. "That's show-biz talk for 'good luck.'"

"Let's hurry," Jessica said as she and Elizabeth unlocked their bicycles outside the school. "It's almost five thirty, and I want to beat Dad home so we don't have to answer a lot of questions about where we've been all afternoon."

"OK," Elizabeth agreed, pulling her backpack over her shoulders. She climbed on her bike and sighed heavily.

"What's the matter?" Jessica asked. "Still feeling guilty about what we're doing?"

"Not too guilty," Elizabeth admitted. "That was a sigh of relief. I'm actually beginning to think we can pull this off."

"Me, too," Jessica agreed happily. "And I'm beginning to think we might have a lot of fun, too." Her eyes sparkled. "Just think: It's going to be the biggest night of our lives. We're starring in the talent show. Lila is having a party in our honor with all kinds of important people. To top it off, we're going to be in a movie. And if we actually win first prize in the talent show, we'll get season tickets to the L.A. Lions soccer team." She shrugged happily. "I don't care about not being psychic if I can still be a star."

Elizabeth shook her head. "I just want to get through this."

"Jessica! Elizabeth!"

Elizabeth looked up and saw Randy Mason pedaling in their direction.

"Hi, Randy," Elizabeth said as he pulled up next to them on his bike.

"Hi," he panted. "What are you guys doing here at school so late?"

Elizabeth darted a nervous look at Jessica. But Jessica didn't look at all ruffled. "Just doing a little studying," Jessica answered calmly.

"Don't you think you guys should be home resting?" Randy asked. "I mean, the talent show is tomorrow, and it's probably pretty hard to be psychic if you're tired. At least that's what my uncle told me."

Jessica gave him a smug look. "I guess that's true—*for amateurs*," she said with a superior smile.

Don't push it, Elizabeth warned her mentally. Not that she thought it would work.

Randy grinned. "I can't wait to see you guys in action tomorrow night. The whole school is talking about it. In fact," he added, "some of the guys were talking about you at lunch today. They're trying to get up enough nerve to ask you about their love lives."

"Tell them we'll be happy to help," Jessica offered.

Elizabeth glowered at Jessica. Sometimes she wanted to strangle her sister. They'd just managed to get themselves out of one hole, and now Jessica was trying to dig them into another one.

Elizabeth leaned over on her bike and dug her elbow into Jessica's ribs.

"Ooomph!" Jessica looked at Elizabeth and caught the warning look in her sister's eyes. "Just tell the guys that we'd be happy to help . . . *but* we've discussed it thoroughly and decided that it's not a good idea to use our psychic power for anything frivolous."

Good save! Elizabeth thought, flashing a little smile at Jessica.

Randy nodded. "Sure. I can see that. This is pretty serious stuff. You know, maybe you should offer your services to the government." He gazed at them with a solemn expression. "You could talk to my uncle about it. He takes this stuff pretty seriously, and he knows a lot of people in Washington. In fact, that's where he is right now."

Elizabeth felt her stomach knot.

"You mean your uncle isn't in town yet?" Jessica asked anxiously. "The talent show is tomorrow."

"He'll be here," Randy assured her. "He's flying to Sweet Valley tomorrow afternoon. But he has to be in Washington tomorrow morning."

"What's he doing in Washington?" Elizabeth asked, even though she was pretty sure she was happier not knowing.

"He's the state's witness in a federal trial of a phony psychic," Randy answered.

Elizabeth gasped and felt the color draining from her face.

"What's the matter?" Randy asked.

Elizabeth nervously licked her lips. "I don't feel so good," she answered.

"I don't blame you. I'll bet phony psychics make you guys just as sick as they make my uncle," Randy said.

"Right," Elizabeth squeaked.

"My uncle says the phonies mess up things for the people who are for real—and that's why the police and the CIA don't take the real ones seriously. If they *did* take them seriously, the police and the CIA could solve a lot more crimes."

Elizabeth gulped. This was awful. It was one thing to fool people at a middle-school talent show. It was another thing to mess with the CIA.

"I hope your uncle really nails that psychic," Jessica said angrily.

"Jessica!" Elizabeth whispered.

But Jessica was off and rolling. "I hope your uncle gets that psychic put away for a long time, so he can't ruin the reputation of other, for-real psychics, like me and Elizabeth."

"Jessica!" Elizabeth croaked.

"Phony psychics should be locked up for life!" Jessica finished, stamping her foot.

Randy nodded. "That's exactly what my uncle says. And that's why he says he's going to be watching you two very closely."

"Oh," Jessica said softly.

Nine

◇

"What's the matter with you girls?" Mr. Wakefield asked that night at dinner. "Neither one of you has said a word. And Elizabeth, you've hardly touched your dinner."

Elizabeth looked up guiltily. She'd been too busy worrying about Randy's uncle to talk or eat.

Mr. Wakefield smiled. "I know I'm not the greatest cook in the world, but I promise you, there's nothing poisonous in those hamburgers."

Steven laughed and stuffed the remainder of his hamburger in his mouth. "The chow is great, Dad!" he said with his mouth full.

Mr. Wakefield looked at Steven and shook his head. "Thanks for the compliment. But could you please not talk with your mouth full?"

"Sorry," Steven said, taking a big swig of milk.

Mr. Wakefield looked over at Jessica and his eyebrows shot up. Elizabeth turned to stare at her twin too.

Jessica's face was twitching. Her eyes blinked. Her nose wrinkled. Her brow furrowed. And her eyebrows lifted.

"Jessica. Is something wrong with your face?" Mr. Wakefield asked.

Jessica dropped her fork with a clatter. "No!" she said quickly. "Why do you ask?"

Elizabeth frowned. She knew her sister was practicing the code. If Mr. Wakefield could spot it, Randy's uncle was *bound* to spot it too. *That's it,* Elizabeth decided. *This just confirms what I've been worrying about all evening.*

"Am I losing my mind tonight?" Mr. Wakefield asked. "Or is it the three of you?"

"What do you mean, you won't do it?" Jessica yelled, pacing across Elizabeth's carpet.

Elizabeth sighed. "If Dad spotted it, Randy's uncle will spot it in a minute."

"Don't be such a big chicken!" Jessica argued. "Sure, it's obvious, now. But it's like Maria said— all the movements are normal facial gestures. We just have to be more subtle."

"We just have to forget the whole thing," Elizabeth countered. "And even if Randy's uncle didn't spot us—which he would—it's still dishonest and phony."

"Elizabeth!"

"It's wrong, Jessica. You heard Randy. Phony psychics undermine the credibility of real psychics. That's why the police and the CIA don't take them seriously."

"Well, they *shouldn't* take them seriously," Jessica said. "Because I'll bet they're all just as phony as we are. If you look at it that way, we're doing the *right* thing. We're making the world a safer place by keeping the police and the CIA from wasting their time with people like us."

Elizabeth narrowed her eyes and glared at Jessica. "I hate it when you do that."

"Do what?"

"I hate it when you twist things around and make stuff that's stupid and wrong sound logical and moral."

Jessica laughed. "But we *will* be doing the right thing, Lizzie. People are paying money to be entertained. We have an obligation to entertain them."

"I don't care," Elizabeth said stubbornly. "I won't do it. I won't use the code."

"How can we go on without using the code?" Jessica groaned.

"We'll just have to do the best we can," Elizabeth said.

"*The best we can!* That's crazy. *The best we can* stinks!"

"Being phony stinks even worse."

"We're phonies whether we use the code or not," Jessica pointed out.

"Yeah, but at least we're *honest* phonies."

"Now who's twisting things around?" Jessica demanded.

As Elizabeth watched, Jessica's lower lip began to quiver and her eyes began to look watery. "I can't believe you're really going to do this to me," she said in a shaky voice.

Elizabeth crossed her arms over her chest. She wasn't falling for Jessica's crying act again.

A large tear rolled down Jessica's cheek. "Please, Elizabeth!"

Elizabeth felt a heavy lump in her stomach. Those looked like real tears on Jessica's cheeks. She really was upset. Elizabeth watched as her sister buried her head in her hands and her shoulders began to shake.

For one brief moment, Elizabeth reconsidered. But suddenly she saw Jessica sneak a quick peek at Elizabeth's face, to see if she was falling for it.

"No dice!" Elizabeth said curtly. "You're faking."

Jessica's expression immediately changed from sad to angry. She stood up and stamped her foot. "Fine! Just fine," Jessica said hotly. "After tomorrow night I'm never going to speak to you again—*ever*!"

Jessica stomped out of Elizabeth's room and shut the door with a bang.

Elizabeth ran to the door and jerked it open. "And after tomorrow night," she shouted, "I never want to hear the word *psychic* again!" She slammed the door shut with another bang.

Jessica flew into her room and slammed her own door. But she still wasn't satisfied. So she went over to the bathroom door, opened it, and slammed *it* shut—three times in a row.

Bang! Bang! Bang!

Then, just in case Elizabeth didn't realize how angry she was, she slammed it shut again.

Jessica paced furiously around her room in circles. Darn Elizabeth! Why did she always have to be such a goody-goody? Why did she always have to be so honest? Couldn't she see how humiliating this thing was going to be for all of them?

Jessica went over and rummaged through her drawer for a nightgown. She quickly took off her clothes and pulled the nightgown on over her head. Then she went over to her dressing table and stared glumly at her reflection.

She was probably going to have to leave Sweet Valley after tomorrow night. She'd probably have to change her name and her appearance and go to a new school where nobody had ever heard of her or Elizabeth.

Jessica swept her hair off her face and held it behind her head. Hmmm. If she cut it really short and dyed it black, maybe nobody would recognize her.

Then she sighed and let her hair fall back down around her shoulders. She didn't want to leave

Sweet Valley. She didn't want to move to a new town and have a new name. What she wanted, more than anything else in the world, was to stay in Sweet Valley and be the most important Unicorn in the club.

She'd been close to getting her wish, too. And just when she thought fame and fortune were finally hers, Elizabeth had come along and snatched it out of her hands.

"Ohhh!" she fumed, throwing herself facedown on her bed. "I just hope you know what you're getting us into, Elizabeth Wakefield. Tomorrow night is going to be the most awful, humiliating, sickening night of our lives. And I hope you lie awake all night worrying about it—just like I know I'm going to."

"Ohhh!" she groaned again, drumming her feet against the bed in frustration.

"Ohhh!" Elizabeth moaned fitfully, turning over in her bed. She was only half awake, and the half-asleep part of her brain kept jumping forward to the following night.

She was standing up on the stage of the Sweet Valley Middle School auditorium, with Jessica beside her. Jessica had her fingers pressed to her temples, and she was ooohing and aahhhing, trying desperately to put on a real show.

Maria stood onstage with a stack of index cards. "What kind of food is Jessica thinking about?"

Elizabeth squeezed her eyes shut and tried as hard as she could to see what was in Jessica's mind. But the only image that popped into Elizabeth's mind was a big ham.

"Ham?" Elizabeth asked in a terrified voice.

Maria slowly turned the index card to face the audience. It said, "Chicken."

"Ohhhhh," Elizabeth said in a disappointed voice. "I thought for sure she was thinking about a ham."

"The only ham around here is onstage!" Bruce Patman shouted from the audience.

"And the only chicken around here is *you*," Jessica muttered at her under her breath.

"Booooo!" the audience yelled.

"They haven't gotten one question right," Janet Howell called out.

"Booooo!" the audience yelled again.

"They're phonies!" Randy Mason shouted from the wings.

A man with a video camera balanced on his shoulder pointed toward the girls with a menacing frown. "Arrest them!"

Suddenly, policemen began streaming up the aisle of the auditorium. "You're under arrest!" one of them shouted as he climbed up onto the stage with two pairs of handcuffs.

"For being phony psychics?" Jessica wailed.

"No. For being boring entertainers," the policeman answered.

The handcuffs closed with a snap over the girls' wrists.

The whole audience jumped to their feet and booed and hissed.

"Lock them up and throw away the key!" Ellen Riteman shouted.

"Lock them up! Lock them up!" the audience began to chant.

"It's all your fault," Jessica wept to Elizabeth as the policemen pushed them out of the thundering auditorium. "It's all your fault!"

Elizabeth jerked awake with a gasp. *Thank goodness it was only a nightmare*, she told herself as she tried to calm down.

But then she was struck by a terrible thought. Tomorrow night, that nightmare was going to come true. She jumped out of bed and ran through the bathroom into Jessica's room.

"Yeow!" Jessica shrieked as Elizabeth landed on her bed with a thump.

"Wake up!" Elizabeth demanded.

Jessica sat up, turned on the light, and glared at her. "I *am* awake. I've been awake all night. And I wish you'd stop running into my room and jumping on my bed like that. Why can't you just knock like everybody else?"

"Sorry," Elizabeth said breathlessly. "But I just had a horrible nightmare about tomorrow night."

Jessica smiled. "Really?"

Elizabeth nodded.

"Good," Jessica said cheerfully. "I've been lying here all night hoping that you would."

"Thanks a lot," Elizabeth snapped.

"It serves you right," Jessica snapped back. "Now get out of my room so I can try to get some sleep." She reached over to turn out the light, then flopped back against the pillows. "I want to get a good night's rest before the most awful day of my whole life."

Elizabeth reached over and turned the light on again. "I've changed my mind."

Jessica sat up in the bed. "You have?"

Elizabeth swallowed hard and nodded. "Now get up and let's work on that code."

"You mean it?"

"I mean it."

"You're not going to back out again?"

"Jessica! Don't you trust me?"

Jessica chewed on her lip for a moment. "Well, I am a little worried that you're going to have another conscience attack. I'm not sure I can trust somebody as honest as you are."

Elizabeth held out her hand. "Here, I'll shake on it. That means you have my word. And you know I always keep my word."

Jessica's face brightened and she grabbed Elizabeth's hand. "That's right," she said with a smile. "You always do keep your word. I guess that's the upside of having a goody-goody for a sister."

Ten

"I can't wait to see the show tonight," Lila said. "My dad says ticket sales are fantastic. The auditorium is practically sold out."

It was Friday afternoon, and the twins were standing on the front steps of the school with some of the Unicorns.

"I can't wait for your party tonight," Kimberly Haver added. "It sounds totally glamorous."

"Is it going to be a big party?" Mary Wallace asked.

Elizabeth smothered a tired yawn behind her hand. She was glad school was finally over. It had been hard staying awake for her classes. She and Jessica had stayed up practically the whole night practicing the code.

They both knew it backward and forward now,

and they could make all the gestures look like normal movements of their faces. Elizabeth felt pretty confident that they could pull it off, but even so, she was dreading it.

"It's going to be a very big party," Lila confirmed. "This talent show is really getting people's attention. Daddy invited lots of local TV people, and a bunch of them accepted. The guy from Channel Ten News is coming. He told Daddy that he wouldn't cross the street to see a kid play the violin, but he's really interested in seeing two psychics."

Lila, Kimberly, Mary, and Jessica all squealed with excitement, but Elizabeth's heart sank. This just seemed to get worse and worse.

"Will there be lots of food?" Kimberly asked.

"Tons of it," Lila said. "My dad hired a caterer, and they're serving really fancy stuff, like shrimp and liver paté."

Elizabeth wrinkled her nose.

"That sounds totally sophisticated." Kimberly sighed. "And just think, Jessica, you and Elizabeth are the guests of honor."

"Just think," Elizabeth said wryly. Jessica glared at her and dug her elbow into Elizabeth's ribs.

"I'll bet Ellen Riteman is just furious," Tamara said.

"She is," Mary Wallace confirmed. "I talked to her this morning, and she's telling everyone that Jessica and Elizabeth are phonies. She said she's going to be watching you guys very carefully to make sure you don't pull something funny."

Elizabeth felt her face growing pale. But Jessica flashed her most superior smile. "Poor Ellen. It must be awful to be such a mean, jealous person."

"Just be glad she's not the star attraction anymore," Kimberly said. "She could have really made the Unicorns look ridiculous."

"And Jessica is going to make us famous," Tamara said happily. "We're really proud of you, Jess."

Jessica beamed proudly. Elizabeth rolled her eyes.

"Uh . . . we really need to get home and . . . and get our costumes together," Elizabeth said, desperate to get out of there.

"She's right," Jessica said reluctantly. "We'll see you guys tonight at the show."

"You guys are great!" Mary yelled after them.

Us guys are phonies, Elizabeth thought unhappily.

"Can you believe it?" Jessica said as they hurried home on their bicycles.

"No!" Elizabeth said angrily. Her nerves were practically stretched to the breaking point. "I can't believe that I actually let you drag me into this. I'm getting more and more nervous every second. All those people that Lila invited are professional show-biz types. They're bound to spot us using the code."

"Would you relax?" Jessica begged. "We worked on those facial gestures for hours last night. Nobody's going to be able to spot what we're doing at all."

Elizabeth sighed.

"Are you having a conscience attack?" Jessica asked, a worried expression on her face.

"No. I'm having an anxiety attack," Elizabeth shot back.

"Whew!" Jessica said with a smile. "That's a relief."

"That looks great!" Jessica exclaimed.

Elizabeth went over to the mirror. In spite of her growing anxiety, she couldn't help smiling at her reflection. She really did look like a psychic. They both did.

They had cut stars and moons out of metallic paper and pinned them onto their long, silky dresses. Then they had each made themselves a turban out of a scarf, and finished off the whole effect with long, dangling earrings and an armful of bangle bracelets.

Elizabeth darted a nervous look at the clock. "OK," she said, pulling the scarf off of her head. "I've got to go drop something off at the Regent Hotel for Mom. You take this stuff over to the school, and I'll meet you there before the show."

Jessica frowned. "What are you doing at the Regent Hotel?"

Elizabeth flushed guiltily. "Well, don't tell Mom this, but I was supposed to take a letter and a check to the banquet manager at the Regent Hotel on Monday. But with all this stuff about the talent show going on, I forgot about it. I talked to the guy yesterday, and he told me I could bring it to him today at five."

"But the show starts at seven," Jessica protested. "We're supposed to be backstage by six."

"I'll be there," Elizabeth promised. "All I have to do is run in, drop off the envelope, and then get over to school. I'll probably be there *before* six." Elizabeth noticed that Jessica was still frowning. "What's the matter?" she asked.

Jessica shook her head. "I don't know. I just have a strange feeling that I shouldn't let you out of my sight."

"Why?"

"I'm afraid you'll chicken out on me."

"*Jessica!*" Elizabeth exploded. "Have I ever broken a promise to you?"

"Nooo," Jessica said thoughtfully. "But you've never forgotten to do something important for Mom, either."

Just then, Steven appeared in the doorway. "Quick," he challenged, "tell me what I'm thinking about."

"Food!" both girls said at the same time.

He smiled. "Wow. You guys look like the real thing."

"We are the real thing," Jessica replied huffily.

"I hope so. You can't believe how many Sweet Valley High people are going to this thing. If you guys bomb tonight . . ."

"We're not going to bomb!" Jessica insisted through gritted teeth. "Are we, Elizabeth?"

Elizabeth swallowed and shook her head. "No," she said in a hoarse whisper.

"Good," Steven said, walking away.

"Where are you going?" Jessica called out.

"To the kitchen," Steven answered.

"See!" Jessica shouted. "You *are* thinking about food! I *told you we were psychic!*"

"Hello?"

No one answered. "Hello?" Elizabeth called out again, a little louder this time.

She looked around the deserted lobby of the old Regent Hotel in confusion. There was nobody in sight. No one was behind the front desk, and the shops off the front lobby were locked up and dark.

Boy, Elizabeth thought. *This is spooky. Spooky and weird.*

Elizabeth looked at her watch. It was five o'clock. And this *was* the Regent Hotel. So where was everybody?

"Is there anybody here?" she called in a wavering voice.

"In here," a distant voice answered.

"Where are you?" she called out.

"In here. Through the double doors."

Elizabeth followed the sound of the voice and discovered that it was coming from the direction of the big dining room. She stepped inside cautiously and gasped. It looked like the inside of a haunted house. All the tables and chairs were draped in white sheets, and the high-backed dining-room chairs looked like ghosts.

"Can I help you?"

Elizabeth jumped in startled surprise and whirled around. Then she let out a sigh of relief. It wasn't a ghost. It was a painter. He wore paint-speckled overalls, and held a brush.

He gave her a friendly smile. "Looking for somebody?"

"I'm looking for Mr. Peters," she replied.

"Right. He told me to keep an eye out for you. He's in his office on the tenth floor. Just take the elevator in the lobby."

The painter dipped his brush in a coffee can full of turpentine and then wiped it with a rag. "You can go on up." He smiled and put the brush down on a pan. "And I can go home now. Mr. Peters asked me to wait until you got here before I left. He was afraid you wouldn't know where to go."

"Thank you for waiting," Elizabeth said.

"No problem," the painter responded. "Have a nice weekend."

Elizabeth hurried out to the lobby, found the elevator, and pushed the button.

The old elevator began to creak and hum, and Elizabeth heard the car descending slowly from an upper floor toward the lobby.

Come on. Come on, Elizabeth thought impatiently. It was well after five now, and she knew she had to hurry.

Finally the elevator arrived. Elizabeth jumped into the car and pressed the button for the tenth floor.

The doors closed with a loud creak.

The Regent was a landmark building. Lots of people thought it was quaint and picturesque, but Elizabeth couldn't help wishing they had a more up-to-date elevator. This old thing was taking forever.

After what seemed like an hour, Elizabeth stepped out of the elevator onto the tenth floor. Across the hall she saw a door that had "Banquet Office" stenciled in gold letters, and pushed it open. The outer part of the office was empty. "Mr. Peters?" she called out.

A nice-looking man stepped out of an inner office. "Elizabeth Wakefield?"

"That's me," she said with a smile, holding out the letter. "Here's the stuff from my mom."

"Thank you, dear," he said, taking the letter from her. "I'm sorry you had to wait until today to bring it over, but I was afraid there wouldn't be anybody at all here yesterday to let you in."

"What's going on?" Elizabeth asked. "Where are all the guests, and the staff, and everything?"

"We always close for three weeks this time of year," Mr. Peters explained. "The staff takes their vacation, and we do whatever refurbishing is required—painting, repairs, things like that. Tell your mom not to worry, though. We'll be open in plenty of time for the designers' banquet."

Mr. Peters looked at his watch. "Wow. It's getting late, and I need to get moving. I'm just going to change the message on the answering machine. There won't be anyone here until Monday. I'm leaving town, and the painters don't work on weekends."

"I've got to get going too," Elizabeth said. "I'm supposed to be at school by six for a talent show. Thanks a lot for letting me bring this over so late."

"No problem. Do you want me to see you out? Everyone else is gone. And I know the lobby can seem pretty scary when it's empty."

"Oh, no." Elizabeth smiled. "That's OK."

"All right, then. You have a nice evening."

"I'll try," Elizabeth said, hurrying out the door and back into the hall.

She pressed the button for the elevator. She heard the distant creak and hum as the gears began to operate.

She waited . . . and waited . . . and waited.

She shifted from one foot to the other. She'd never get to school if the darned elevator didn't hurry up.

Elizabeth glanced over to her right and spotted a

door with a red Exit sign. *Ah ha! Steps!* Taking the stairs would be a lot faster than waiting for the elevator.

She hurried over to the door and pushed it open.

Bang! The door clanged shut behind her as she began to hurry down the stairs.

She rounded the landing on the tenth floor, then the ninth, then the eighth. She was running now, hopping down the steps and taking them two at a time.

Fifth floor . . . fourth floor.

She turned the corner of the third-floor landing sharply, holding on to the handrail. By the time she reached the ground floor she was out of breath. She lifted her hand to shove the door open and . . .

Her stiff arm bounced off the door, and she stumbled back.

That's funny, she thought. Then she realized that the door probably opened in, rather than out. She put her hand on the doorknob and tried to turn it. But it didn't even budge.

She grasped the knob tighter and gave it a hard shake. "Open up," she ordered. The doorknob still didn't turn. Obviously, this door was locked.

Elizabeth turned and ran up to the second floor. She put her hand on the knob and tried to open the door. It was locked too!

Sweat broke out across Elizabeth's forehead. *I'm not going to get nervous yet*, she told herself as she ran up to the third floor.

She put her hand on the knob and turned. It didn't move either. She tried again. Nothing. *Darn!*

Elizabeth hoisted her backpack higher on her shoulders and ran up to the fourth floor. But that door was locked too.

Elizabeth worked her way back up to the tenth floor, stopping on every landing. Every single door was locked. The tenth floor was her last chance.

She put her hand on the door and squeezed her eyes shut. *Please open! Please!* But it wouldn't open either.

Maybe if she banged and yelled, Mr. Peters would hear her. Elizabeth lifted her fist and pounded on the door. "MR. PETERS!" she shouted. "I'M LOCKED IN THE STAIRWELL! CAN YOU HEAR ME?"

She pressed her ear to the door and listened. But there was no response. Elizabeth pounded on the door again.

Bam! Bam! Bam!

"MR. PETERS! IT'S ME, ELIZABETH WAKE-FIELD. I'M LOCKED IN. CAN YOU HEAR ME?"

Elizabeth's heart began to pound. Mr. Peters must have left already. He'd probably ridden down in the elevator while she was in the stairwell.

A sob rose in her throat, and Elizabeth swallowed hard. *I'm leaving town, and the painters don't work on the weekend,* he had said.

The hotel was empty. And she was locked in until Monday morning.

Eleven

"Where *is* she?" Maria demanded.

"I don't know!" Jessica moaned, pacing around the crowded area backstage.

It was pandemonium behind the big curtain of the Sweet Valley Middle School auditorium, and Jessica practically had to shout to be heard.

Tumblers and gymnasts, including Amy Sutton, were flipping and cartwheeling in every direction as they warmed up for their acts. Anna Reynolds and Jo Morris were practicing their modern dance routine. Two eighth-grade jugglers threw Indian clubs, milk cartons, and even stuffed animals back and forth to each other. A kid with a ventriloquist's dummy gargled with a throat full of water while his dummy sang "Yankee Doodle Dandy." Julie Porter played scales on her flute. Tamara

Chase and Mandy Miller were practicing their dance steps to a Melody Power song blaring from a boom box, and moving their hands around to illustrate the lyrics.

Ms. McDonald, the music teacher who was in charge of the show, came hurrying over to Jessica. "Where is your sister?" she demanded. "All students participating in the talent show were supposed to be here at six o'clock sharp. It's almost seven o'clock."

"I know, Ms. McDonald. And I'm sorry. But she'll be here soon. I know she will. I have her costume all ready for her. All she has to do is run in and put it on."

"Please let me know the minute she arrives," Ms. McDonald said in a harried voice. She looked down at her clipboard and shook her head. "We've already lost one act at the last minute. The skateboarding rapper fell off his skateboard this afternoon, and broke his wrist *and* his jaw."

"Oh, no," Jessica said.

Ms. McDonald nodded grimly. Then she made a note on her clipboard and hurried away.

So that's why Tamara and Mandy are rehearsing so hard, Jessica thought. *They're going to get to go on after all*.

"Hey, Jessica!" Amy Sutton was waving to her from the other side of the area backstage. Then she jumped in the air and did back-handsprings across the floor, landing with a thump at Jessica's side.

"Wow!" Maria breathed. "That was great!"

"Thanks," Amy said with a proud grin. She looked around. "Where's Elizabeth?"

"I don't knoooow!" Jessica groaned. "And if one more person asks me, I'm going to scream."

Amy frowned. "It's almost seven o'clock. All the acts were supposed to be here by six."

"I know," Jessica said.

"Maybe she's at home," Amy suggested.

"I just called. There's no answer. My dad and Steven were going to the airport this afternoon to pick up my mother. Then they were going to come directly to the school."

"Where in the world could she be?" Maria cried in frustration. "You guys are the main attraction. If Elizabeth doesn't show up, a lot of people are going to be very disappointed."

"I know one person who won't be disappointed," Amy muttered under her breath, darting her eyes toward Ellen Riteman.

Ellen stood alone, holding her sheet music in her hand. "Mi mi mi mi miiii . . ." she warbled weakly.

"Amy Sutton!" a voice called out. "Please come take your place in the lineup!"

Amy gave Jessica and Maria a grin. "It's showtime!"

Jessica bit her lip nervously and adjusted her turban. "I know," she said hoarsely.

"Don't worry," Amy said. "She's probably just

running late. You've still got lots of time before your act goes on."

Amy cartwheeled away. Jessica let out a long sigh.

Maria sighed too, and adjusted the bow tie that made her black pants suit look like a tuxedo. "Uh, Jessica," she said slowly. "You don't think that Elizabeth . . ."

". . . chickened out?" Jessica finished for her.

Maria nodded.

"No way!" Jessica said in a firm voice, even though deep inside, she was afraid that her sister might have had another conscience attack.

"Excuse me," a deep voice interrupted. "Are you Jessica or Elizabeth Wakefield?"

Jessica turned and saw a man with a video camera peering curiously at her down his long, beaky nose. "I'm Jessica Wakefield," she answered.

The man's eyes narrowed and he studied her face intently. "I'm Cliff Mason," he said finally. "Randy Mason's uncle."

"The filmmaker!" Maria exclaimed.

"Documentarian," Mr. Mason corrected gravely. "This is a very important film I'm working on. And I just wanted to thank you and your sister for giving me an opportunity to film a couple of real psychics at work. Getting here involved a lot of big scheduling problems, but I'm always ready to go to any lengths to get a true psychic on film."

Jessica's heart began to thud. Mr. Mason

sounded pretty serious about this. He *looked* pretty serious too. In fact, he looked like a man who probably *enjoyed* prosecuting phonies.

He gave her a sinister smile. "I hope I haven't wasted my time." He nodded curtly. "Good luck!"

"Geez! That guy's kind of scary," Maria commented as Mr. Mason strode toward the wings of the stage.

Jessica nodded, almost beginning to wish that she had chickened out herself.

"Looks like the Psychic Sisters are short one sister," she heard a raspy voice comment. She looked over and saw Ellen sneering at her.

"Elizabeth'll be here," Jessica said with more confidence than she felt. "Is there something wrong with your voice?" she asked sweetly.

"There's nothing wrong with my voice!" Ellen retorted. "It's a little tired from rehearsing, but it's going to be fine. *I* will be going on as planned, unlike some people."

"We'll be going on," Jessica shot back. "Don't you worry."

"You can't go on without Elizabeth," Ellen pointed out. "And she's not here. I'll bet she chickened out, didn't she? I was talking to Randy this afternoon. He told me about how his uncle helps to put phony psychics in jail." Ellen gave Jessica a knowing smile. "I'll bet that's why Elizabeth isn't here. You guys are phonies, and she's afraid Randy's uncle is going to find out."

Jessica's heart did a flip-flop. If anybody around here was psychic, it was Ellen.

"Elizabeth had to run an errand before the show," Jessica explained nervously. "She's just a little late, that's all."

"*Hah!*" Ellen barked in a very loud, gruff voice. Then something strange happened. Her hand flew to her throat and her eyes opened wide in horror.

"Ellen? What's the matter?" Maria asked quickly.

Ellen opened her mouth and tried to talk. But all that came out was a feeble squeaking sound.

"Ellen! Are you all right?" Jessica asked.

Ellen pointed frantically to her throat. "Mmm . . . vv . . . ce . . ." she managed to say.

"Your voice?" Jessica said.

Ellen nodded. "G . . . n . . ."

Jessica's eyes widened. "Your voice is gone!"

Ellen nodded again, and then glared at Jessica. "Y . . . r . . . f . . . lt."

"My fault!"

Ellen nodded again and pointed her finger at Jessica. "W . . . tch."

"I am *not* a witch!" Jessica argued. "I'm a psychic. There's a big difference."

But Ellen was backing away, pointing her finger accusingly. "W . . . tch."

"I am not a witch, Ellen. You just went *hah* really loudly. It probably blew your vocal cords."

"W . . . tch," Ellen croaked one last time, before hurrying away.

Jessica rolled her eyes. This night was getting weirder and weirder. *The minute Elizabeth gets here,* Jessica thought grimly, *I'm going to kill her.*

Then she had an idea. Maybe Elizabeth was still at the Regent Hotel. Maybe the guy she was supposed to see had kept her waiting.

Jessica ran toward the door that led to the hallway.

"Where are you going?" Maria shouted.

"To make a phone call," Jessica answered.

A few minutes later, Jessica replaced the receiver of the pay phone in the hall. Her legs wobbled and she had to lean against the wall to keep from falling down.

Closed for renovations, the recording had said.

Jessica could hardly believe it. Elizabeth had lied to her. Made up a whole big story about going to the Regent Hotel.

How could she have gone to the Regent Hotel *when it wasn't even open*?

"Can *anybody* hear me?" Elizabeth shouted desperately. She knew that yelling and screaming was a waste of time. But she just had to keep trying. It kept her from imagining what her starved and lifeless body would look like on Monday when she was found.

She looked at her watch. Seven o'clock.

"Arrgggghhh!" she screamed out loud. "This is

the most horrible thing that's ever happened to me in my whole life!"

Elizabeth sat down on a step and dropped her head into her hands. It was awful being all by herself in the dimly lit stairwell of the deserted hotel. The only light came from a naked bulb that hung from the ceiling by a long cord.

And there were strange sounds that made her heart flutter. Weird noises that made her think about ghosts.

Elizabeth stood quickly before her imagination took over and ran completely wild. "HELP!" she cried. "SOMEBODY PLEASE LET ME OUT OF HERE!"

Jessica peeked out from behind the curtains. The auditorium was full to capacity. She could see her parents and Steven in the third row, laughing and applauding as if nothing in the world were wrong, as if Jessica weren't about to face the most absolutely humiliating experience of her entire life.

"Jessica!" Maria tugged on her sleeve. "Now that Ellen's dropped out they've pushed all the other acts up. It's going to be your turn soon. I hate to say this, but I don't think Elizabeth is going to show up."

A hot tear began to trickle down Jessica's cheek. She couldn't believe it. She just couldn't believe Elizabeth would do something this cruel.

She's paying me back for all the awful things I've ever dragged her into, Jessica thought miserably. *I should have known this was going to happen. I should have known she'd back out. She said she thought it was wrong. And this is her way of teaching me a lesson.*

"We've got to figure out what we're going to do," Maria hissed. "Any ideas?

Jessica shook her head, and her lip began to tremble. All she knew was that her sister had abandoned her. And for the first time in her life, she couldn't come up with a single, solitary idea. Not one.

Elizabeth's lip trembled. She was tired. She was cold. She was hungry, too. But the thing that was making her the most miserable of all was thinking about Jessica.

Hot tears began to trickle down her cheeks. Jessica would have to face that audience alone. She would think that Elizabeth had backed out at the last minute. And she'd be so mad about it, she wouldn't even think to tell anybody to come looking for her here.

The single light bulb began to flicker ominously.

"Oh no!" Elizabeth whispered. "Please don't go out. I don't want to be all alone here in the dark."

Elizabeth stared hard at the light bulb, willing it to stay on. If only she really *were* psychic, she could send Jessica a message telling her she was trapped here in this horrible stairwell.

Elizabeth shut her eyes and concentrated as hard as she could. Maybe . . . just maybe . . . there was something to this psychic business after all. *And if there is,* she thought desperately, *please let it work now.*

Twelve

"Jessica!" Mandy said in an awed whisper. "Did you really put a spell on Ellen?"

Jessica sat backstage on a stool, staring glumly into space and thinking about Elizabeth. "Don't be ridiculous," she mumbled.

"Because if you did, it's the best thing you could have done for the Unicorns—and for us."

"That's right," Tamara confirmed. "Now Ellen won't go on and make a fool of herself. And we get to go on and do *two* numbers to fill in for the two missing acts."

You may get to go on and do three numbers, Jessica thought miserably.

She looked over and saw Ellen Riteman standing tearfully in the shadows. Her heart sank and she couldn't help feeling sorry for Ellen. If Ellen felt even half as bad as Jessica did right now, then she was feeling pretty awful.

Jessica sat up straighter on her stool. In a few minutes, she was going to go down in flames. Do a big-time crash and burn in front of a huge audience, an L.A. filmmaker, and several people in the television business.

She remembered the French Revolution and the picture in the book. She had an idea. Maybe she should make one last noble gesture before her life was over.

She stood and lifted her chin. "Mandy," she said, "haven't you ever noticed that most girl singing groups have *three* members?"

"So?" Mandy asked.

Jessica made a grand, sweeping gesture with her arm and pressed her fingertips against her forehead. "My psychic abilities tell me your act will be a bigger hit if you let Ellen go on and lip-synch with you guys."

Mandy blinked. "Well. Gee. OK. If you say so."

Mandy and Tamara hurried over toward Ellen. As Jessica watched, Ellen actually began to smile.

"Lip-synchers!" Ms. McDonald called out. "You're on next!"

Mandy, Ellen, and Tamara hurried toward the stage.

"Remember me well," Jessica whispered, as she watched her fellow Unicorns take their places in the spotlight.

* * *

"WE WANT THE PSYCHIC SISTERS. WE WANT THE PSYCHIC SISTERS. WE WANT THE PSYCHIC SISTERS! WE WANT THE PSYCHIC SISTERS!" The audience was shouting and stamping their feet.

"Jessica!" Ms. McDonald said with a sigh. "We simply cannot put your act off any longer. Now, what do you want to do?"

Maria squeezed Jessica's shoulder. "It's now or never," she whispered.

Jessica's heart was aching. Those people were clapping and cheering and screaming for her and Elizabeth. It should have been the most exciting night of her life, and Elizabeth had ruined it for her.

Jessica would have loved to turn and run away. But over to her left, she saw Randy's uncle positioning himself and his camera in the wings.

There was nowhere to run.

"WE WANT THE PSYCHIC SISTERS! WE WANT THE PSYCHIC SISTERS! WE WANT THE PSYCHIC SISTERS!" shouted the audience.

Jessica pulled her turban into place and took a deep breath. "Well," she said grimly to Maria. "I'm going to have to go out there and just do my best to apologize to everybody."

Maria gave Jessica a sympathetic look. Then she patted Jessica on the shoulder and turned sadly away.

Jessica threw back her shoulders and stood. She

was trembling when she stepped out onto the stage.

"Yeah! All right!" members of the audience shouted.

Jessica smiled weakly and lifted her hands for silence.

The audience immediately became quiet.

"Ladies and gentlemen!" Jessica began, her voice sounding high and tinny. "Thank you so much for that warm reception."

There was another burst of applause.

Out of the corner of her eye Jessica saw Randy's uncle aiming his camera at her. Automatically, she gave a broad grin to the camera.

Then she looked back out at the audience. She saw her parents. She saw Steven. It made her angry and sad all over again. She could understand how Elizabeth might do something like this to her—but she couldn't understand how Elizabeth could hurt Steven, too.

Elizabeth sat in the cold stairwell, shivering with fright. The light bulb was flickering on and off now. *Oh, please,* she thought. *Please somebody remember where I am!* She stared hard at the bulb. *Please, Jessica. Remember where I am!*

Jessica looked back in the direction of Randy's uncle, and suddenly a light bulb went on in Jessica's brain.

When my uncle heard that story about Elizabeth being trapped in the basement, he flipped! she heard Randy's voice saying in her head.

Trapped! The word reverberated back and forth in Jessica's mind.

What had she been thinking? Elizabeth wouldn't do something this mean to Steven *or* Jessica. Never in a million years. If Elizabeth said she was going to the Regent Hotel, then that's where she had gone. Obviously, something had happened to her at the hotel. Somehow, she'd gotten stuck there. Somehow, she'd gotten *trapped.*

Jessica put her hand to her forehead dramatically. "Ohhhhhh!" she moaned.

She rocked back and forth, as if she felt faint. "Ohhhhhhh," she moaned again.

She couldn't resist sneaking a peek at the camera to make sure Randy's uncle was getting it all.

"DO SOMETHING PSYCHIC!" someone in the audience shouted.

Jessica opened her arms wide and swayed. "Hellllp! Hellllllllp!" she sang in a high, shrill voice.

Then Jessica shook her head, as if she were trying to clear it. "Excuse me, ladies and gentlemen. I'm sorry, but I'm getting a psychic message from my sister."

"Where is your sister?" someone shouted.

"Shhhhhhhh!" several people in the audience hissed.

Jessica couldn't help smiling. She had their

attention now—and she planned to keep it.

She let her head fall back. Her eyes closed and her mouth fell open. "Jesssicaaaa. Jeessssssicaaaaa! Can you heaaarr meee?"

Jessica lifted her head and put on an alert expression. "Where are you, Elizabeth! Is something wrong?"

"Hellllpp!" she whimpered, in what was supposed to be Elizabeth's voice.

Jessica opened one eye and saw her parents. They looked very confused. Mrs. Wakefield whispered something to Mr. Wakefield, and Mr. Wakefield shook his head and shrugged. Then they both whispered something to Steven, and he shrugged too.

Talk about a surprise act! Jessica thought happily. *I just hope I'm right.*

Jessica shook herself from head to toe. Then she put her hands to her head as if she had a sudden, terrible pain. "Ladies and gentlemen," she said again. "I came out here to apologize to you for the absence of the other Psychic Sister. Up until just a few moments ago, I had no idea where she was. But as I'm sure you all heard, she's sending me a psychic message. She's in trouble—I'm not sure what kind, but it's serious trouble."

"Where is she?" someone shouted.

Jessica raised her eyes to the ceiling and lifted her arms. "ELIZABETH! CAN YOU HEAR ME! WHERE ARE YOU!"

Then suddenly, Jessica reeled back. "Ohhhhhh!" She spun around on the stage, and then she let her head and shoulders go limp again. "I'M AT THE REEEeeegeent HOOOoooootellll!" she said in Elizabeth's voice.

"Is this some kind of a joke, Jessica?"

Jessica opened her eyes and saw her father standing next to the edge of the stage. He looked worried and angry.

"No," Jessica said quickly. "Elizabeth is in trouble. And I'm pretty sure she's trapped at the Regent Hotel."

The people in the audience began to shift in their seats and murmur.

The next thing Jessica knew, Mrs. Wakefield and Steven had joined Mr. Wakefield at the edge of the stage. "What's going on?" Steven whispered.

Randy's uncle came over to join them and began filming their family conference.

"Who are you?" Mr. Wakefield demanded.

"Cliff Mason, documentarian. I'm here to get this psychic event on film."

Mr. Wakefield look annoyed and rolled his eyes. "I don't know what this is all about," he snapped, "but we're going to the Regent Hotel right now." He reached up, put his hands around Jessica's waist, and swung her down off the stage.

"Hey!" Jessica protested. "I haven't finished my act."

"I'm finishing it right now," her father said,

124

striding up the aisle and tugging her along behind him.

"What's going on?" a man shouted from the front row.

"Where is she going?" a lady complained.

"They're going to rescue her sister," Cliff Mason shouted out, panning his camera across the audience.

Jessica waved her arm in a big dramatic gesture. "Thank you all. You've been a *wonderful* audience. And I—"

But she didn't get to finish, because her father grabbed her arm and yanked her out of the auditorium.

Jessica smiled at the camera. She was sitting in the back of the Wakefields' car with Randy's uncle. Outside, on the dark street, a police car sat parked with its lights flashing.

"We're outside the Regent Hotel," Randy's uncle was saying in a low, dramatic tone, providing the voice-over for his tape. "The police have just arrived."

Jessica adjusted her turban and grinned into the camera again.

"Jessica waits in breathless suspense, while the police attempt to open the locked front doors of the deserted hotel," Mr. Mason said.

Immediately, Jessica changed her facial expression to what she hoped was breathless suspense.

She opened her eyes wide and her mouth formed an "O."

"A second police car has arrived," Randy's uncle said, as the lights of another police cruiser illuminated the street. "Jessica worries that that means trouble," he added in a low, tense voice.

Jessica changed her facial expression to puzzled worry. She furrowed her brow and turned the corners of her mouth down.

"Wait!" Randy's uncle said. "Another car is arriving."

Jessica turned her head in time to see a brown sedan pull up behind the second police car. A man wearing a blue blazer got out and hurried over to greet Mr. and Mrs. Wakefield.

"Maybe that's the banquet manager," Jessica said.

"Maybe it's the banquet manager," Mr. Mason repeated in a dramatic voice.

His delivery made Jessica wish she'd said it with a little more punch. "Can I do that line again?" she asked.

Mr. Mason lowered the camera. "This is a documentary, Jessica. Not a feature film. The point is to get things down the way they actually happen."

"Sorry," Jessica said.

Mr. Mason opened the car door and began to climb out.

"Where are you going?" Jessica cried.

"I want to get this on film," Mr. Mason explained.

"Wait for me!" Jessica hurried behind him toward the group gathered at the front door of the hotel.

"Why! There's your little girl," the man in the blazer said in surprise when he saw Jessica.

"This is Jessica, Mr. Peters," Mr. Wakefield explained. "It's her twin sister that's missing."

"And from what Jessica's told us, we think she may be somewhere in the hotel," Mrs. Wakefield said.

Mr. Peters pulled a set of keys from his pocket and unlocked the front door of the hotel. "I'm happy to let you folks look around. But I'll tell you the same thing I told the police: She left just before I did, and she said she was on her way to school."

"But she never arrived!" Mr. Mason intoned, aiming his camera at the group in the doorway.

Mr. Peters frowned in confusion. "Who are you?"

"Cliff Mason. Documentarian. I'm here to get this psychic event on film."

"Oh!" Mr. Peters said. "I see." But Jessica could tell by his expression that he had no idea what Mr. Mason was talking about.

Mr. Peters opened the front door, and Jessica followed her parents and the police into the pitch-black lobby.

"Let me get the lights," Mr. Peters offered.

A few seconds later, the bright lobby lights came on. Jessica looked around and shivered. There was something spooky about the empty hotel lobby. It looked so ghostly and deserted.

"The lobby looks ghostly and deserted," Mr. Mason said into his camera mike.

"Hey, that's exactly what I was thinking," Jessica said, looking directly into the camera. "I was even thinking those exact same words. See?" She grinned, tapping her turban. "Psychic!"

"ELIZABETH!" Mr. Wakefield shouted.

The four policemen spread out through the lobby, peeking into doorways.

"ELIZABETH!" Mrs. Wakefield shouted.

Elizabeth strained her ears. She thought she heard something.

"Elizabeth!" she heard her mother's voice call faintly through the heavy door.

"IN HERE!" Elizabeth shrieked, her heart hammering in her chest. "I'M IN HERE!" She lifted her hand and pounded on the door, tears of relief springing to her eyes. "I'M IN HERE. LET ME OUT! OH, PLEASE! LET ME OUT!"

The door flew open and she saw Jessica silhouetted against the light. "JESSICA!" Elizabeth shouted, throwing herself into her sister's arms.

"Elizabeth, honey!" Mrs. Wakefield cried, as she hurried toward the two girls and hugged them both.

Mr. Wakefield appeared right behind her.

Elizabeth was overjoyed to see her parents. But

she was even more overjoyed to see Jessica. "I knew it," Elizabeth cried. "I knew you'd figure out I was here. I knew you wouldn't let me down. I sent you a psychic message and it worked. It really worked!"

"I knew you wouldn't just back out on me!" Jessica cried. "I knew you had to be in trouble." Then she turned quickly and grinned at Mr. Mason's camera. "See?" she said, tapping her turban again. "Psychic!"

Thirteen

"And now," the Channel Ten newscaster was saying, "we're going to tell you the story of an amazing rescue that took place tonight."

Jessica and Elizabeth sat in front of the big-screen television that was positioned in the middle of the Fowlers' enormous living room. All of the party guests were gathered around them, holding plates of shrimp and paté. But nobody was eating—they were all captivated by what they were watching.

On the screen, a picture of Sweet Valley Middle School appeared. "Jessica and Elizabeth Wakefield were scheduled to appear this evening in the Sweet Valley Middle School Talent Show. The purpose of the show was to raise money for the Sweet Valley Children's Hospital. But Elizabeth Wakefield never arrived at the school."

"There you are!" Tamara Chase squealed.

Jessica giggled as she saw herself up on the stage of the school auditorium. "Heelllllp meee!" she was moaning.

Elizabeth burst out laughing. "Jess!" she whispered in her sister's ear. "How corny."

"Shhhh!" Jessica hissed. "Watch."

"Elizabeth's twin, Jessica, went onstage alone at eight thirty. At first, she feared her twin had failed to appear due to stage fright. But at eight thirty-two, Jessica says she received a *psychic message* from Elizabeth." The newscaster gazed solemnly at the camera. "The message she received led Jessica to believe that her sister was trapped at the Regent Hotel."

On the screen, they saw Mr. Wakefield pulling Jessica out of the auditorium. "Jessica and her family immediately left the school talent show and contacted the police."

The picture changed to Mr. and Mrs. Wakefield, Steven, and the police greeting Mr. Peters. "The police were able to reach the banquet manager of the hotel at his home, just minutes before he was about to leave town for the weekend."

On the screen they saw Jessica and Elizabeth hugging each other in the stairwell. "Once inside the deserted hotel, they located the missing Wakefield twin, who was, indeed, trapped in the stairwell."

The picture changed to a huge close-up of

Jessica. "See?" She grinned, tapping her turban. "Psychic!"

Jessica disappeared from the screen, and the newscaster smiled into the camera. "Psychic phenomenon? Who knows. It could just be a case of two sisters who care enough about each other to always believe the best. Jessica says she knew Elizabeth would never let her down. And her sister, Elizabeth, says the same thing about Jessica. Psychic or not, it's an exciting story of sisterly love and eleventh-hour rescue. Thanks for tuning in. Good night!"

All the guests at the party burst into applause, and Jessica and Elizabeth hugged each other again.

"You guys are amazing!" Lila said, as Janet, Mandy, and Tamara formed a circle around Jessica and Elizabeth, and the adults drifted into groups to chat. "My dad says this story will probably be picked up by all the national news channels and magazines. It's going to get great publicity for the hospital."

Elizabeth smiled. "Well, I'm glad *some* good came out of this."

Mandy shook her head. "I don't get it. How did the news channel get all that film and everything? How did they put the story together so fast?"

"Mr. Mason hurried from the hotel over to the television station," Jessica explained. "He said he couldn't use the tape for his movie, but he did sell it to the news people, and it covered his expenses for the trip. He also said he was going to sell it to that show called *Real-Life Rescues*. So we may get to be on a *national* TV show, too."

Janet patted Jessica on the back. "You did it, Jessica. You put Sweet Valley Middle School on the map, you made the Unicorns look great, you generated publicity for the hospital, *and* . . ." she darted a look around to make sure that Ellen wasn't listening, ". . . you put a spell on Ellen that kept her from singing. Why didn't you tell us you were a . . ." Janet lowered her voice to a whisper, ". . . witch?" She shook her head. "You really do have amazing powers, Jessica."

Tamara nodded solemnly. "Just think of all the really great stuff you can do."

Jessica's mind was racing. If her friends thought she was a witch, she would really have it made. She could boss everybody around as much as she wanted. She might even get to be president of the Unicorns.

"Do you think you could teach me some spells?" Lila asked eagerly.

"Well," Jessica said. "I suppose I could. But . . ."

Just then, Jessica noticed Elizabeth's face. Elizabeth looked so angry that her brows were practically connected over her nose.

"Jessica!" she said in an ominous voice.

"But . . . Elizabeth and I talked it over, and we've decided to retire our supernatural powers forever," Jessica finished quickly.

Elizabeth smiled and nodded. "Unless, of course, the CIA or the police need us."

Steven stood by his dad and Mr. Fowler, and stared glumly at the growing number of kids who were gathering around his sisters.

"Ned," Mr. Fowler said with a laugh, "I hope you're proud of your daughters. Their act certainly was . . . *unusual!*"

Mr. Wakefield laughed. "Life with the twins is always unusual! Just be glad there's only one of Lila."

Steven groaned. "I still can't believe it. I can't believe that their act totally bombed but they still managed to turn it into a big success and get on television. How come stuff like that always happens to them and never happens to me? They are so lucky, it's sickening."

Mr. Wakefield laughed. "Would it cheer you up to hear that I managed to get some tickets to an L.A. Lions game next week?" he asked.

Steven brightened immediately. "It sure would." Then he had a horrible thought. "Wait a minute! Speaking of tickets, who won those season tickets? If you tell me the twins won, I'm going to run away from home."

Mr. Fowler put his hand on Steven's shoulder. "Don't worry. The ventriloquist won the soccer tickets."

Steven let out a sigh of relief. "Phew. If the twins

had gotten this much attention and won the tickets, too, I'd *never* hear the end of it."

Mr. Wakefield laughed. "You don't mind if they come to the soccer game with us, do you?"

"I guess not," Steven said. "They really like soccer."

"Lila seems to have developed an interest in soccer recently too," Mr. Fowler commented. "Soccer must be the latest craze."

"It's getting really popular," Steven confirmed. "Even at the middle-school level. I heard the middle-school boys might even have a shot at competing in Division A."

Mr. Wakefield whistled in surprise. "In that case, something tells me we're going to be hearing even *more* about soccer over the next few weeks."

What will happen when the soccer craze hits Sweet Valley Middle School? Find out in Sweet Valley Twins No 71, JESSICA SAVES THE TREES.

We hope you enjoyed reading this book. If you would like to receive further information about available titles in the Bantam series, just write to the address below, with your name and address: Kim Prior, Bantam Books, 61–63 Uxbridge Road, Ealing, London W5 5SA.

If you live in Australia or New Zealand and would like more information about the series, please write to:

Sally Porter   Kiri Martin
Transworld Publishers   Transworld Publishers (NZ) Ltd
(Australia) Pty Ltd   3 William Pickering Drive
15–25 Helles Avenue   Albany
Moorebank   Auckland
NSW 2170   NEW ZEALAND
AUSTRALIA

All Bantam and Young Adult books are available at your bookshop or newsagent, or can be ordered from the following address: Corgi/Bantam Books, Cash Sales Department, PO Box 11, Falmouth, Cornwall, TR10 9EN.

Please list the title(s) you would like, and send together with a cheque or postal order to cover the cost of the book(s) plus postage and packing charges of £1.00 for one book, £1.50 for two books, and an additional 30p for each subsequent book ordered to a maximum of £3.00 for seven or more books.

(The above applies only to readers in the UK, and BFPO)

Overseas customers (including Eire), please allow £2.00 for postage and packing for the first book, an additional £1.00 for a second book, and 50p for each subsequent title ordered.

SWEET VALLEY TWINS

Don't miss the extra-long special editions of this top-selling teenage series starring identical twins Jessica and Elizabeth Wakefield and all their friends.

SUPER EDITIONS

SUPERCHILLERS

SWEET VALLEY HIGH

The top-selling teenage series starring identical twins Jessica and Elizabeth Wakefield and all their friends at Sweet Valley High. One new title every month!

<table>
<tr><td>1. DOUBLE LOVE</td><td>55. PERFECT SHOT</td></tr>
<tr><td>2. SECRETS</td><td>62. WHO'S WHO?</td></tr>
<tr><td>3. PLAYING WITH FIRE</td><td>63. THE NEW ELIZABETH</td></tr>
<tr><td>4. POWER PLAY</td><td>67. THE PARENT PLOT</td></tr>
<tr><td>5. ALL NIGHT LONG</td><td>68. THE LOVE BET</td></tr>
<tr><td>6. DANGEROUS LOVE</td><td>69. FRIEND AGAINST FRIEND</td></tr>
<tr><td>7. DEAR SISTER</td><td>70. MS QUARTERBACK</td></tr>
<tr><td>8. HEARTBREAKER</td><td>71. STARRING JESSICA</td></tr>
<tr><td>9. RACING HEARTS</td><td>72. ROCK STAR'S GIRL</td></tr>
<tr><td>10. WRONG KIND OF GIRL</td><td>73. REGINA'S LEGACY</td></tr>
<tr><td>11. TOO GOOD TO BE TRUE</td><td>74. THE PERFECT GIRL</td></tr>
<tr><td>12. WHEN LOVE DIES</td><td>75. AMY'S TRUE LOVE</td></tr>
<tr><td>13. KIDNAPPED</td><td>76. MISS TEEN SWEET VALLEY</td></tr>
<tr><td>14. DECEPTIONS</td><td>77. CHEATING TO WIN</td></tr>
<tr><td>15. PROMISES</td><td>78. THE DATING GAME</td></tr>
<tr><td>16. RAGS TO RICHES</td><td>79. THE LONG-LOST BROTHER</td></tr>
<tr><td>17. LOVE LETTERS</td><td>80. THE GIRL THEY BOTH LOVED</td></tr>
<tr><td>18. HEAD OVER HEELS</td><td>81. ROSA'S LIE</td></tr>
<tr><td>19. SHOWDOWN</td><td>82. KIDNAPPED BY THE CULT!</td></tr>
<tr><td>20. CRASH LANDING</td><td>83. STEVEN'S BRIDE</td></tr>
<tr><td>23. SAY GOODBYE</td><td>84. THE STOLEN DIARY</td></tr>
<tr><td>24. MEMORIES</td><td>85. SOAP STAR</td></tr>
<tr><td>26. HOSTAGE</td><td>86. JESSICA AGAINST BRUCE</td></tr>
<tr><td>27. LOVESTRUCK</td><td>87. MY BEST FRIEND'S BOYFRIEND</td></tr>
<tr><td>29. BITTER RIVALS</td><td>88. LOVE LETTERS FOR SALE</td></tr>
<tr><td>30. JEALOUS LIES</td><td>89. ELIZABETH BETRAYED</td></tr>
<tr><td>35. OUT OF CONTROL</td><td>90. DON'T GO HOME WITH JOHN</td></tr>
<tr><td>40. ON THE EDGE</td><td>91. IN LOVE WITH A PRINCE</td></tr>
<tr><td>44. PRETENCES</td><td>92. SHE'S NOT WHAT SHE SEEMS</td></tr>
<tr><td>49. PLAYING FOR KEEPS</td><td>93. STEPSISTERS</td></tr>
<tr><td>54. TWO-BOY WEEKEND</td><td>94. ARE WE IN LOVE?</td></tr>
</table>

Created by FRANCINE PASCAL

Jessica and Elizabeth Wakefield have had lots of adventures in *Sweet Valley High* and *Sweet Valley Twins* . . .

Now read all about the twins at age seven! All the fun that comes with being seven is part of *Sweet Valley Kids*. Read them all!